Call My Bluff

Call My Bluff

ERIN CHESNUT

The Cypress Valley Sweethearts Series

BOOK TWO

Call My Bluff

Copyright © 2025 by Erin Chesnut

ISBN 979-8-9902820-1-8

Editing: Mild Mannered Editors
Cover and interior design by Alt 19 Creative

This one is for every version of myself that thought I might be delusional—from the early years to the very, very recent. Look at us now. We did it! (Again.)

OTHER BOOKS IN
THE CYPRESS VALLEY
SWEETHEARTS SERIES

Fight for Me
Jake and Lexie's story

(Available in all formats on Amazon and Audible.
Signed copies available on Etsy.)

AUTHOR'S NOTE

I knew before I started this book that it would be a bear to write. Most of the other books in the Cypress Valley series have already started drafting themselves in my head; I have pages and pages of notes and backstory and possible scenes already waiting to be fleshed out. But for this one, all I knew was that Olivia and Noah needed each other, and that it needed to happen before their college graduation.

That's it, that's all I had, and I don't know how many times I asked myself if this story was really necessary. Maybe I should toss it all in the trash and skip to book three and be done with it; maybe I should circle back to Olivia later and somehow bring Noah back into her life; maybe they weren't meant to be together at all and I'm just trying to fit a square peg into a round hole. But every time I tried to walk away, they called me back. I love both their personalities so much, and they demanded to have their story told. So here we are at last, on THEIR terms, and I pray it's everything you hoped it would be.

Dear Reader,

In my books you can expect warm fuzzies, flirtatious banter, sizzling kisses and a happy ending without explicit scenes or foul language. However, deeper themes sometimes emerge, so if you do not need or appreciate content warnings, please skip the next paragraph and dive right into chapter one.

This book contains brief mentions of a father who leaves his family (past) and an implied reference to a child who has been abused (mentioned in the context of a social worker's job).

Erin Chesnut

1

NOAH CAMPBELL WATCHED from the corner of his eye as Simon Provo, the store's self-anointed "Customer Service King," made his way toward his office in the corner. Noah kept his body turned toward his work, as if he weren't paying attention, while his victim moved out of sight.

Three . . . two . . . one . . .

An inhuman scream split the air, followed by a tremendous crash. "Get it away!!" Simon screeched, his voice two octaves too high.

Noah bit down on his bottom lip, eyes clenched tight, as he fought the urge to laugh.

"Somebody help me!" Simon screamed again, and two other managers came racing from the aisles toward the source of the commotion.

Noah's friend Riley leaned across the end of her register. "What did you do?" she hissed, but he shook his head violently. He couldn't speak—not while the sounds of battle raged inside the small office behind him.

That bag of rubber snakes was worth every penny.

"Kill it! Kill it!" Simon shrieked. Then there was a pregnant sort of pause. "What do you mean *it's not real?!*"

That was the last straw. Noah's body shook with the effort of holding in his laughter, and tears started to leak down his cheeks.

"He's going to kill you," Riley whispered, though her voice trembled with her own amusement.

"He has to prove it was me first," Noah muttered back. He sucked in a deep, cold breath and did his best to make his face behave; he was only partially successful.

"What's all that about?"

A young woman's voice caught his attention, and he turned to see a customer approaching Riley's checkout stand. She wasn't one of their regulars; no, Noah knew them all, and this girl he would have remembered. She was all bold colors and curved lines—from her reddish-brown hair to her green skirt, which stopped just above a pair of black, knee-high boots. She looked like she'd just come from a photo shoot for '50s pinup posters.

"It seems our manager had an unwanted visitor," Noah answered, finally bringing his voice under control. "No reason to worry, though. You're safe with me." He shot her the kind of grin that normally made girls blush, but this one simply raised an eyebrow in response.

"That seems doubtful," she deadpanned, and Riley snorted.

The angry voices from the office grew louder, and there was another ominous crash. Riley began scanning the girl's purchases, and Noah packed them in bags as fast as he could. "Can I walk these out for you?" he asked as he lowered the sacks into the girl's now-empty cart.

She swiped a debit card and waited for her receipt. "You mean you don't want to stay and watch the fallout?" she asked.

"I'll catch the reruns," he replied quickly, stepping behind her cart and closing his hands around the handle. "Besides, we give carryout service with a smile!" He started toward the exit just as the occupants of the office emerged.

Simon's hair was on end, his face still red, and one of the other managers was holding a *very* realistic-looking rubber rattlesnake by the tail. The poor thing had somehow been hacked to bits in the melee, and its head was hanging by a thread.

Noah passed through the automatic doors without looking back; either the girl would follow her groceries, or she wouldn't, but he was getting out of Dodge just the same.

Footsteps hurried up behind him a moment later.

"A snake? Really?" the girl asked as she drew even with him.

Noah felt an incriminating smile stretch across his face. "I don't know what you're talking about," he said as innocently as he could.

"Sure you don't."

There was a moment of silence as they walked farther across the parking lot. Noah waited for some indication they were approaching her car, but none came.

"You know this is pointless, right?" she finally asked.

"What is?"

"The whole 'grocery store carryout' thing. I mean, I appreciate the gesture, I guess, but I've got to haul these up three flights of stairs when I get home. *That's* when I'd rather have help," she said.

"Well, you could take me home, but you'd have to buy me dinner first," he quipped, diving headfirst into the opening she'd given. It was too good to waste. The girl huffed, but Noah saw the edges of her mouth twitch like she was trying to control a smile. "Assuming you still need dinner after all this candy," he added. "Please tell me this will last more than a day." He waved his hand toward her groceries, which included chocolate pretzels, gummy bears, half a dozen pints of ice cream and the biggest bag of Pixy Stix he'd ever seen.

The girl turned her head toward him as they walked, her eyebrows raised. "It's breakup food, actually," she said, and Noah's ears perked up.

"Oh, really? I'm sorry. Do you need a hug?"

The girl rolled her eyes, her lips pursed, but Noah decided she was definitely laughing on the inside at least, though *with him* or *at him* was yet to be determined.

"It's not for me, but nice try," she said. "My roommate just had a nasty episode with her boyfriend, who I hope is a soon-to-be ex. Most of this is for her."

Noah let out a low whistle. "Must have been pretty bad to need a hundred Pixy Stix and half the freezer section," he said. He turned to look at the girl again and saw dark storm clouds pass across her face.

"Let's just say I wouldn't be opposed to castration with a rusty kitchen knife, should the opportunity arise," she said dryly.

Noah barked out a surprised laugh. "Wow. You gonna do it yourself?" he asked, only half kidding. A girl's willingness to maim a man seemed like something a guy should know from the beginning.

"I know people," she answered darkly, and Noah made a mental note not to get on her bad side. She reached into her shoulder bag and pulled out a small key ring before pressing a button on the fob.

He heard the chirp of locks nearby, and the trunk of a dark-purple Mustang GT popped open. He surveyed the car with a twinge of jealousy. "Nice ride," he said as he brought the grocery cart to a stop. He slowly loaded the first of her bags into the trunk, certainly in no hurry to head back inside.

"Thanks," she replied. She reached into one of the remaining grocery sacks and popped a hole in the package of Pixy Stix. Then she slid a red one away from the others before tearing off the end and dumping the powdered candy into her mouth.

Noah noticed a Cypress Valley State University parking sticker on the bottom corner of her back window, and he nodded toward it as he added a second bag to her load. "You go to CVSU? I don't think I've seen you shop here before. What's your name?"

"Yeah, I'm a senior, and I don't, normally. But I was in the area, and my roommate is in desperate need of a sugar rush, so here I am," she replied.

Noah loaded the last bag and reached up to close her trunk. "You didn't tell me your name," he pointed out, unwilling to let that omission slide. "If you don't, I'll just have to make something up."

The girl turned away before popping open her driver's side door and tossing her purse inside, but she didn't climb in after it. Instead, she leaned one hip against the car's frame and regarded him with something akin to curiosity. "Oh, really? And what would you make up for me?" she asked.

Noah thought hard, watching the way her eyes danced as she waited for an answer. His gaze flitted from her outfit to her car and back to the paper tube still in her hand. "Pixie," he said, knowing the second it left his lips he'd never call her anything else. His chest expanded in triumph as a slow grin spread across her face.

The girl folded the now-empty candy wrapper between her fingers and laughed. It was a bright, musical sound, just as Noah had somehow known it would be, and he almost did a victory dance.

"I like it," she said, taking a few backward steps. "Points for creativity, Grocery Boy."

Noah moved away as she ducked into the driver's seat and snapped her door shut. The pavement rumbled beneath his feet as the Mustang roared to life, and both her front windows rolled down to welcome the autumn air. A classic rock station blared from her speakers as she pulled a pair of aviator sunglasses from above the front visor and slipped them on, obscuring his view of her hazel eyes, though he could still feel her gaze on his skin.

"Good luck with your snake problem!" she shouted over the music. Then she waved as she put her car in reverse.

"Thanks," he replied, unsure if she could even hear. The car pivoted past him and then shot from the lot, leaving him standing in a literal cloud of dust. He could hear the roar of her engine even after she'd driven out of sight, but it couldn't erase the way her laughter still rang in his ears.

Noah could feel the wheels turning in his mind—which was usually what got him into trouble. She hadn't told him her name, but that would only make the hunt more challenging.

And he had never backed down from a challenge.

2

THREE WEEKS LATER, Olivia parked her car down the street from a sprawling ranch-style house and peered at the scene beyond her windshield. There were plastic folding tables along both sides of the paved driveway and across the front yard, all covered in teetering piles of miscellaneous junk.

She smiled, already feeling anticipation flooding her veins. There was something about a good garage sale that funneled her usual chaotic energy into a single, focused mission: to find that perfect *something*. Sometimes it was a vintage dress, sometimes a killer pair of barely worn heels, sometimes a fringed lamp that matched her curtains and accent rugs. She never knew what she was going to find, but the excitement of not knowing was half the fun.

Olivia climbed out of her car and tucked a folded wad of cash into the pocket of her jersey running shorts. The already-fallen leaves of a nearby oak tree crunched under her sneakers as she made her way along the curb and then turned up the driveway. The first table on her right held stacks of vinyl records, and she began to sort through them. She didn't own a record player, but that wasn't the point; the point was to hunt—and hunt she would.

Half an hour later, she'd worked her way up part of the driveway and across the lawn, snagging a framed piece of stained glass along the way. She was considering the merits of a purple soap dish shaped like a hippo when she finally saw *it*.

An overstuffed, emerald-colored love seat.

It was *perfect!*—exactly the right pop of color for her neutral-heavy apartment.

She wandered purposefully through the last table displays, careful not to look too eager. Finally, she paused where the love seat waited at the mouth of the two-car garage, her head cocked to one side as if still deciding. In reality, she was already mentally rearranging her furniture.

"Hello," said a female voice, and an older woman in denim shorts and a neon-green racerback approached. "Are you interested in the love seat?"

Olivia pursed her lips and forced herself not to answer right away. "Maybe," she hedged, pulling out her phone. "How much are you asking?"

"One fifty even," the woman replied. She rearranged a few items on a nearby table as she spoke. "It's clean and in good condition; no pet hair or stains, and it's from a nonsmoking household. One fifty is a steal."

It *was* a steal, considering Olivia had seen a similar piece on sale for $499 at a local furniture store. But this was not her first rodeo. "I'm not sure it will fit in our place," she stalled. "Do you know the dimensions? I'll talk to my roommate."

The woman rattled off some numbers while Olivia alerted her best friend.

OLIVIA: I found us a couch! It's green.
Should fit under the window. I'm gonna
need a truck.

LEXIE: Where are you?

OLIVIA: 537 Harolds Court

LEXIE: I'll get Jake. Work your magic!

Olivia nodded politely to the woman, who was still standing nearby. "Let me think about it," she said.

"Of course! Take your time," the woman replied, and she walked away to help an older lady with a lamp.

Olivia moved to a shelf of tiny porcelain figurines, all the while scanning the sparse crowd of shoppers. The best person to talk to at a sale like this was the seller's husband; he was usually anxious to get his garage back and willing to send the junk on its way with minimal fanfare. She looked for anyone who might fit the bill. There were several middle-aged women sorting a stack of tea towels and one young mother watching her children rummage through a bin of stuffed animals. A younger guy was inspecting a rusty bicycle frame leaning against the side of the house, but there were no other men in sight.

She shifted from one foot to the other. If Jake Tanner wasn't running to his pickup truck at that very moment, she'd eat her shoes! The poor boy had only been dating her best friend for two weeks, but he was already wrapped around her pinkie finger about as tightly as he could be.

Sure enough, her phone buzzed in her hand a few seconds later.

> **LEXIE:** On our way! Jake's picking me up, and he's bringing one of his roommates. We owe them pizza.

Olivia chuckled softly. Yep, that's what she'd thought.

A set of door hinges squeaked to her left, and an older gentleman with a receding hairline stepped out of the house and onto the smooth garage floor. Olivia looked along the length of the driveway and saw the woman she'd spoken to standing at the far end discussing something with the mother and her kids.

It was time to make her move.

"Excuse me, sir!" she called, lifting her hand to catch the man's attention. "Are you selling this couch?"

The man looked around, as if surprised to find someone speaking to him, and gave her an uncertain sort of smile. "Well, my wife is. I'm not sure what she's asking for it, honestly. It's been in the garage for a while."

Perfect.

"Hmm," Olivia said, pretending to consider. "Well, I could have some friends pick it up today, if we can afford it. What do you think about . . . seventy-five?"

The man rubbed one hand across the scruff on his chin and looked nervously out toward the yard. "I think she wanted a bit more than that. I can go get her for you."

"Oh, that's okay. I don't want to bother anybody," Olivia answered quickly. "I saw a smaller one at another sale anyway. Thanks, though!" She waved cheerily and started to walk away, hoping with all her might that he valued the empty space in his garage more than a couch he wasn't using anyway.

Thankfully, she was right.

"Wait!" the man called as she stepped into the sunshine, and Olivia barely kept herself from smiling. She turned back to find him half jogging out to meet her. "What about one ten?"

Olivia pulled the folded bills from her pocket and flipped through them, biting her bottom lip for good measure. "I *maybe* could do ninety."

The man winced, but he looked at the money with wistfulness in his eyes. "I'll do one hundred if you can take it today. I just want it gone."

Sold!

But Olivia sighed deeply and counted her bills again. "Alright, but would you put this back for me?" she asked, handing over the stained glass windowpane. The man held up his hands, palms out. "You can have that, ma'am. Just take it."

"Are you sure?" she asked, clutching it to her chest as if he'd just given her the Taj Mahal. "Thank you, sir. I appreciate it!" She handed over her payment and mentally did a victory dance right there in the driveway—and not a moment too soon. The rumble of an engine grew louder, and she saw a blue pickup come to a stop near the end of the driveway.

Lexie opened the front passenger's door and jumped to the ground. "Liv! It's beautiful!" she gushed when she reached the garage. She plopped down onto the generous cushions and wiggled happily. "I think it's full of angel wings."

"I know, right?" Olivia answered, sitting down beside her friend. "Now we just have to get it loaded before the lady who lives here realizes her husband practically gave it to me."

"Oh, don't worry. The boys will have it done in five minutes," Lexie assured her.

Olivia absentmindedly wondered who Jake had brought with

him—probably another soft-spoken cowboy type, like himself. She thought, again, of the boy from the grocery store and wondered if he'd made it through that day alive. She wouldn't be surprised to find out he'd been fired . . . or burned at the stake. His manager had certainly looked angry enough to do it, though it would be a pity if those pretty eyes went up in smoke.

She heard the boy's deep chuckle in her mind for the thousandth time and quickly pushed the memory away. She'd never been in the habit of chasing after boys, and she wasn't going to start now. Graduation was coming, her internship would start next semester, and job application websites were bookmarked on her laptop. This was not the time to complicate her life—pretty eyes or not.

Jake backed the bed of his truck up over the curb, and she watched the taillights flash and go off. Moments later, the rear driver's side door popped open, and Jake's friend slid out. He was wearing light-wash jeans and a dark T-shirt, and a shock of jet-black hair peeked out from beneath a baseball cap. As he came closer, she found herself looking into a familiar pair of blue-gray eyes that sparkled with humor as they met hers.

Apparently, Olivia didn't need to complicate her own life— karma was happy to do it for her.

PIXIE.

Her long hair was tied up in that messy thing girls did when they were trying not to care too much, and she wasn't all made up the way she had been that day in the store, but even from a distance, Noah knew it was her. He made his way up the driveway, watching her as he went, and he saw the moment recognition dawned on her face. Judging by the look in her eyes, she was just as surprised to see him as he was to finally find her.

"You've got to be kidding!" she shouted, her voice exactly as he remembered it—teasing and playful with a hint of mischief underneath.

"Hey, Pixie," he replied, and the grin he'd been holding at bay slipped out. "Looks like you're gonna buy me dinner after all."

The girl huffed out a laugh and rose to stand, but not before Lexie voiced the obvious question. "Do you two know each other?" she asked from her place on the couch.

"Sort of. He stole my groceries once," her friend answered airily. She pulled the cushion she'd been sitting on from the love seat and leaned it against the brick of the house. Lexie pushed to her feet and did the same.

"I wouldn't call it *stealing*," Noah replied.

"You ran off with a cart full of stuff I'd already paid for! That's stealing," Pixie countered.

He twisted his mouth to one side and bent to test the weight of the couch at one end. "I wasn't running; I was walking with purpose."

"You were *escaping*," she pointed out.

"Why did you call her Pixie?" Lexie interrupted, moving out of the way so Jake could grab the opposite end of the sofa.

Noah braced himself, his hands under the edge of the couch as his friend got into position. With a nod of Jake's head, they both lifted, and the four wooden legs left the cement. "Because she wouldn't tell me her name," Noah said with a grunt, focused on not toppling a nearby table. "So I had to think of something."

"To your left," Jake called, directing Noah as they maneuvered along the edge of the driveway.

From the corner of his eye, Noah saw the girls grab their respective couch cushions and start hauling them toward the truck.

"It's Olivia!" Lexie called, and Noah smirked as the other girl shoved her with the cushion. Lexie giggled. "What?" she asked loudly, the words obviously directed at her friend. "He's carrying a *couch*, for goodness' sake! He deserves to know!"

Within minutes, everything was loaded and ready for the ride. Noah gave one of the rachet straps a final yank and looked over to where Olivia was sitting on the corner of the open tailgate.

"I'm Noah, by the way," he said. "Moving man by day, grocery boy by night and Jake's best friend by unfortunate circumstance."

"Unfortunate for *him*, you mean," she quipped, and Noah chuckled.

"Exactly."

Olivia leaned in closer, and he could see the way the colors in her hazel eyes rolled together like clouds before a storm. "You do remember I live on the third floor, right?" she asked, her voice almost a whisper, and he felt a rush of adrenaline that had nothing to do with the forced labor in his future.

"Well, I do now," he replied, and Olivia laughed.

She pushed herself off the tailgate with a little hop and landed squarely on her feet. Then she turned without another word and wandered down the street toward where her Mustang waited along the curb.

Noah stared after her for a moment before letting a wide smile creep across his face.

This girl was gonna be trouble.

"SO, I CAME home to find this guy"—Jake jerked his thumb toward Noah—"smashing holes in his bedroom wall with a hammer."

"I was *hearing voices*!" Noah exclaimed from his seat on the floor. "I thought I was going crazy! You'd be tearing open the drywall, too."

Olivia laughed from the love seat behind him, and Noah felt her socked foot nudge his ribs. "What was it?" she asked.

"A Bluetooth speaker. I found it near the baseboards."

"But why was it there?" Lexie added, piping up from where she sat with Jake on the larger couch.

"Why not?" Jake answered. "The things Noah and Conner do to each other defy logic."

Noah shrugged. It was true.

The small motion made the back of his arm rub against Olivia's shin, and he tried to ignore the heat that radiated through his shirt. She could have moved her leg when he'd sat down. She could have moved it any time after.

But she hadn't, and he was taking that as a good sign.

"I think he had help with this one," he said, narrowing his eyes at Jake. "There is no reality in which I see Conner James doing the army crawl underneath a house."

Jake held up his hands in a sign of surrender. "Hey, man, it wasn't me. I stay out of it," he insisted.

"What else have you done?" Olivia asked, and Noah twisted to look up at where she sat cradling a large yellow bowl of fresh popcorn. The hot, buttery smell wasn't quite enough to erase the fruity scent that seemed to cling to her skin. It was somehow both sharp and sweet—which made sense when he considered the girl wearing it.

He propped one arm up on the couch, his fingers only inches from the bare skin of her leg. He itched to touch her just to see what she'd do. If Jake and Lexie hadn't been there, he might have.

"A little bit of everything, to be honest," he said. "Once, I filled the showerhead with red Kool-Aid powder, and Conner reenacted that famous scene from *Psycho*. Then he filled the air vents in my car with glitter, so I changed all the contacts in his phone to 'Bob Dylan,' and he accidentally sent a questionable text message to his mother. Then he left a life-size blow-up doll in my bed."

"While you were sleeping," Jake added, and Olivia laughed out loud.

"Yeah, I almost wet myself when I woke up," Noah admitted with a sheepish grin. "But Melinda is a wonderful girl. You should come meet her sometime."

"*Melinda?*" Olivia barked, a handful of popcorn frozen halfway to her mouth. "Don't tell me you still have it?"

"*Her*," Noah corrected, "and, absolutely, I do! I'm gonna prop her up by the altar at Conner's wedding."

Jake snickered. "You also duct-taped his bedroom door shut and then assaulted him with a paintball gun when he got out of the shower," he added.

"Yeah, I did do that," Noah replied, still keenly aware of the pressure of Olivia's leg against his side.

"Okay, so explain the snake," she cut in. "First of all, why?"

"Because my manager is a menace," Noah said, as if this were the most obvious answer in the world. "Keeping him humble is my service to society."

"And how do you still have a job?" Olivia asked.

"Because I didn't just waltz into the store with a rattlesnake over my shoulder," Noah explained. "There is no video evidence of me ever having said snake in my possession on store property. He can't prove I left it there, and he knows it. He's been trying for nearly a month."

Olivia nudged her foot against his ribs again. "Sounds like you're the menace."

"I prefer 'vigilante,'" he replied. "Much more mysterious." Then he gave in to temptation and brushed the tips of his fingers against the side of her knee, but Olivia didn't blush or giggle.

She also didn't move away.

Interesting, Noah thought.

He shifted onto his knees and leaned his forearms against the couch beside her, intentionally invading her space—just to see. But she didn't give an inch. "Can I have some of that?" he asked, peering down into her snack bowl.

"No."

The answer was quick—decisive—and from somewhere behind him, Jake barked out a laugh.

"I've seen this on Animal Planet," he said in a loud stage whisper. "She won't share resources, so he'll try to establish dominance . . . Then, she'll eat him."

Noah reached past Olivia and grabbed a throw pillow before chucking it over his shoulder in the general direction of the couch. There was a surprised yelp that must have come from Lexie.

"That's my cue to take the beast home," Jake answered, and Noah turned to see Jake and Lexie rising to their feet. Jake looped an arm around Lexie's shoulders as they made their way to the door. "Five minutes, and then I'm leaving you here," he added, giving Noah a pointed look, though Noah thought he saw the corners of his roommate's mouth twitch with barely suppressed laughter. They walked to the door, and Jake held it open while Lexie went out first.

"Liv is serious about her popcorn," she called over her shoulder. "You'd have better luck laying an egg."

"Bakaw!" Jake shouted, imitating a chicken, and Lexie laughed as the door clicked shut behind them.

The apartment fell silent, and Noah turned back to where Olivia was still sitting motionless on the couch, her bowl clutched protectively in her lap and a bemused expression on her face. He didn't know why, but winning a piece of her treasure suddenly felt essential—like earning the trust of a dragon.

"You know, my mama taught me to share," he pointed out, leaning even closer.

"I asked if you wanted a bowl. You said no."

"Well, maybe I've changed my mind! That's not impossible, you know."

Olivia lifted her brow but said nothing, and Noah fleetingly wondered how she could be so unaffected. He was completely inside her bubble now, his face only inches from hers, and yet she barely seemed to notice.

"Here," she finally said, a trace of laughter in her voice. She retrieved a single fluffy kernel from her bowl and held it out to him, but instead of accepting it outright, Noah opened his mouth and waited. After a moment, Olivia rolled her eyes and tossed the kernel inside. "Now, go home," she said.

Noah crunched her gift happily before rising to his feet. "You're somethin' else, you know that, Pix?"

"Yeah, I'm aware," she said lightly. "And you're out of your league."

Oh, challenge accepted, sweetheart, he thought as he turned toward the door, but his entire body tingled, as if protesting the adding distance. He'd faced the dragon and lived to tell the tale, but he wasn't totally sure he'd come out unscathed.

He also wasn't sure she was wrong.

"ALRIGHT! START TALKING," Lexie demanded, plopping onto the end of Olivia's bed only moments after Jake's truck left the parking lot.

Olivia shook her head, somewhat in awe that her friend had even made it back in the door before starting on the third degree. "What is there to say? I met a guy at the grocery store, he was cute, and it turns out he's Jake's roommate. End of story," she said, fishing through her dresser for a tank top and a pair of pajama pants.

"End of story? Seriously? He has a pet name for you!"

Olivia started to change, not caring that Lexie was still in the room. They'd lived together for four years; there were very few secrets left. "He was making fun of that monster bag of Pixy Stix I bought during the Colt debacle, so, really, that part is your fault," she pointed out, watching her friend's reflection in the vanity mirror.

Lexie crossed her arms but didn't respond.

"Plus, it's nothing. Is he cute? Yes. Is he fun to flirt with? Also yes, but that's the end of it. He's not my type," Olivia said as she pulled the soft flannel pants up her legs.

"*Not your type?*" Lexie repeated. "Let's go through the check-list, shall we?" She began to tick items off on her fingers. "Sense of humor. Unfazed by your attitude. Taller than you. Pretty eyes. Ambitious . . ."

Olivia lolled her head in Lexie's direction and raised one eyebrow.

"Shut up," her friend objected, though Olivia hadn't said anything out loud. "He's planning to be a physical therapist. That's not nothing," Lexie went on.

Olivia made a noise of concession. Her friend was right, as much as she hated to admit it.

"Plus, he's got that James Dean look you like," Lexie said, a teasing note to her voice now. "And there's no reason you had to sit with your leg against his back all night. You just wanted to touch him."

"Objection!" Olivia grumbled. "He was also very warm."

Lexie clapped her hands in delight. "So, you admit I'm right?"

"I admit you have a promising list," Olivia conceded as she ran a brush through her hair. "But he's also the class clown, he knows how good-looking he is, and he'd bat his eyes at anything in a skirt just to get a reaction," she said. "Maybe he does check the boxes, but I'm not interested. In a few years, after grad school . . . maybe. But right now, I have things to do."

"You can do more than one thing at a time, you know," Lexie pointed out. "What is it you told me recently? 'Don't punish yourself for finding something good?'"

"I'm not punishing myself; I'm just being practical," Olivia countered. She climbed onto her bed and reached for the TV remote.

"Maybe you should be a little less practical . . . *Pixie*."

"Shut up," Olivia muttered, though it was without conviction. She settled herself more comfortably against her headboard and tried not to think about the way Noah's gaze had kept dropping to her mouth and how that fact had made her chest tighten. A warm flush crept up the back of her neck, and she hoped with all her might that Lexie wouldn't notice. Nothing her friend could say would change the fact that Olivia was right: Noah Campbell was a distraction she didn't need.

Exhibit A? He was already causing trouble, and he wasn't even there.

3

OLIVIA SCRAWLED HER name on the front office sign-in sheet at Mason County Elementary School before following a familiar path down the third-grade hallway. She'd visited several different kids here during her years with the Big Brothers Big Sisters mentorship program, but her longest assignment was with Avery Pinson—a little boy who really just needed a friend.

She paused outside a classroom with colorful ducks on the door and knocked softly before pushing it open. The teacher, an elementary-school veteran named Mrs. Benedict, glanced her way.

"Avery!" the woman called, barely pausing her lesson. She was used to this exchange, which happened every Thursday after lunch.

A little boy with messy red hair rose slowly from a desk near the back, and Olivia furrowed her brow in concern. Avery was always excited to see her; sometimes he even knocked things to the floor in his haste to reach the hallway. But this time, he looked like he'd rather be anywhere else.

"Hey, buddy!" Olivia said brightly when he'd finally crossed the threshold and closed the classroom door behind him. "Are we doing more art today?" Their current project was his submission to the fall art show: an owl made from soda tabs and a small ceramic pot. She'd spent countless visits wielding the superglue while he'd placed each painted metal tab in the perfect spot, building layers of bright feathers that made the tiny planter come to life.

Avery mumbled something incoherent as he shuffled across the tile floor.

"What was that?" she asked.

"I said it's gone!" he repeated, almost shouting the words in the empty hallway.

Olivia stopped dead. "What happened?" she asked in dismay. The owl had been nearly finished the last time she'd seen it. The little boy's eyes teared up, and Olivia immediately threw her arm across his shoulders. "Okay, how about we go to the library?" she asked quickly.

She steered him to the left and pushed open the first door they came to. Then she guided Avery past the reference desk, snatching an unattended box of tissues as she went, and led him into a small courtyard just beyond the wall of windows.

His first tears fell as the glass door shut behind them.

"Hey, it's okay, we'll make it better somehow," she said in an attempt to soothe him. But it didn't work. The tears fell harder and faster, and, while she wasn't supposed to have prolonged physical contact with her young friends, she decided that—in this particular moment—the rules needed to be suspended. She set the tissues on the picnic table and pulled him into a hug. He returned it with surprising force for an eight-year-old, and Olivia had to concentrate on breathing properly.

"She sm-smashed it," he spluttered. The words were wet, as was the front of Olivia's shirt, and she reached awkwardly to one side for the tissues, glad now that she'd thought to bring them.

"Who did?" she asked. She finally managed to pinch a Kleenex between her fingers and pull it from the box, and she offered it to Avery as his grip on her torso loosened.

"My m-mom."

An unsettled feeling blossomed in Olivia's chest. She'd been told years ago that Avery's father was in prison, and she'd heard stories of his tumultuous homelife with his mom. Whatever had happened to the owl, she was sure it hadn't been an accident.

"Do you want to talk about it?" she asked.

Avery's tears slowed, and he mopped his face with the tissue she'd given him. Then, when that was too damp, he lifted the hem of his shirt and scrubbed at his cheeks. "She was mad," he said miserably.

"At you?"

"No, at Dennis."

"Who's Dennis?" Olivia asked. Avery was an only child, at least as far as she knew.

"Her boyfriend," the little boy explained. "She threw my owl at him, and it cracked against the wall. There were p-pieces everywhere. Tabs everywhere."

Olivia stayed quiet, waiting for whatever parts of the story Avery chose to share, but her uneasy feeling solidified into anger. He'd been working on that owl for *months*, carefully collecting can tabs from everyone in the building—students and teachers alike—before painting them by hand and affixing them where he wanted them. Last week, all the bird had lacked were feet.

And this week, it was gone.

"She threw it away," he went on. "She said I should have left it at school." He stared miserably at the ground, and Olivia handed him another Kleenex when the sniffles started again. "I just wanted her to see it," he added.

The angry ball in Olivia's chest grew bigger, and she reminded herself to control her facial expressions as Avery finished drying his eyes for the second time. "I'm so sorry, buddy. I know you were really proud of how it turned out," she said, though she knew it was poor consolation. "We could start another one, if you want?"

"There isn't enough time. The art show is in two weeks," he pointed out.

Olivia felt the weight of his disappointment pressing down on her shoulders and was filled with the need to ease it. "Okay, so what if we start now and you can have it in the spring show? There's another one in April, right?"

Avery considered this. "Yeah. The end-of-year showcase."

"Alright! So we could make it even bigger this time, since we have the extra months to work."

Avery nodded, a little of his normal light returning to his eyes. "But that would take more tabs. It took forever to get the ones I had."

"Well, then it's a good thing college students drink an unhealthy amount of soda, now isn't it?" Olivia added, and she was relieved to see him smile.

"I'll have to find another planter. Maybe Mrs. Franklin has one," he said. Mrs. Franklin was the school's art teacher, and her collection of found objects was probably unrivaled in the state of Tennessee. If anyone had what Avery needed, it was her.

"Let's go look!" Olivia encouraged, and she stood before taking his hand and tugging him to his feet. The energy that should have never left his body seemed to be returning.

"Maybe she has one with holes in it! We could put the eyes on the front instead of on top," he imagined aloud, and Olivia breathed a silent sigh of relief. Maybe this would all be okay—for now.

But that didn't keep the angry embers in her chest from glowing hotter by the second as she pictured Avery's devastation when the first project had shattered. If she had her way, she'd like to throw another planter . . . this time at Ms. Pinson's head.

NOAH STARED AT a color-coded diagram of the cardiovascular system with his eyes slightly out of focus. He'd been memorizing the names of veins and arteries for so long they were starting to blend together in his head. He squeezed his eyes shut and stretched both arms toward the sky, feeling the burn in his upper back.

"You almost done, honey?"

He opened his eyes to find Mrs. Becky, who ran the Redtail Café, wiping down a plastic chair nearby. She looked at him with concern.

"Do you need this table?" he asked, closing his textbook and sliding it closer to his chair. He was the only person at the café, but he'd been done eating for at least an hour. He wouldn't blame her if she needed him to leave.

"No, no, sweetheart. We won't have another rush until at least three o'clock," she explained. "I just think you might need to take a walk or something before you fall onto the floor."

Noah stretched his legs and rotated his ankles. She wasn't wrong.

"What is it today, anatomy or physics? Or both?" Mrs. Becky asked.

Noah smiled. Maybe he studied here a little too often. "Anatomy," he answered, and he dropped his heavy book into his backpack where it leaned against his chair. There wasn't any point in torturing himself any more today. The exam was tomorrow, and either he knew the material by now or he didn't.

Mrs. Becky sidled closer and pulled a red candy bar from the pocket of her apron before sliding it across the tabletop in front of him. "Have some, sweetheart. You work too hard for a man your age," she said, nodding down at the KitKat.

Noah felt a smile bloom on his face. Mrs. Becky had been working the counter at the campus café for a long time, and he had obviously gotten predictable. "Thank you," he said as he tore open the wrapper and bit into the first stick. "And I have to work hard; I can't get by on my looks forever. You, on the other hand . . ."

Mrs. Becky chuckled and snapped her dish towel in his direction. "Get up and go home, silly boy. Stop flirtin' with me."

Noah grinned and finished collecting his things before devouring the last of the chocolate. Mrs. Becky was probably old enough to be his grandmother, but she was always sweet to him, and it was fun to make her blush every once in a while.

She shook her head in a fond sort of way, much like his mother often did. "Go find a girl your own age," she ordered as he slung his backpack over one shoulder, "and not one of those airheads you make eyes at in here!"

Noah huffed out a laugh. It wasn't a horrible suggestion, though the "airheads" he usually spent time with were the ones who didn't expect too much from him, and that was how he liked it. Expectations created attachment, which created relationships, which created the opportunity for someone to get hurt—and they always did. He lived by the philosophy that if he didn't open that door in the first place, he wouldn't have it slammed in his face later—and so far, it was working.

His feet moved on autopilot as he turned toward the parking lot, and his mind wandered back to the only girl who'd been in his thoughts for the past few days. Olivia Cohen was a conundrum. She didn't shut him down, but she also didn't fawn over him the way other girls did. Noah wanted to find out what made her tick, what made her blush, what made her stop and take notice. He wanted to get inside her head and move the gears around until he understood them all.

She reminded him of one of those old-fashioned horseshoe puzzles he'd loved as a kid. They seemed straightforward on the outside—slide the ring off the horseshoe, and he'd be home free!—but once he'd gotten the box open and started moving the pieces around, he'd quickly realized it wasn't as easy as it sounded. He'd spent hours at a time trying to figure out exactly how they worked, and when he'd finally solved one, he'd been on top of the world.

The slam of a car door interrupted his daydream, and Noah looked up to see his thoughts turn into reality. Olivia was stalking across the parking lot as if she intended to set the world on fire. Noah stopped walking and watched cautiously. In his experience, women were like Roman candles—relatively harmless until the fuse was lit. But even then, as long as you could think on your feet and keep the business end pointed away from you, it was possible to come out in one piece.

Unfortunately, it looked like Olivia was already smoking at both ends.

A smarter man might have turned around, but Noah liked to

test the limits of human intelligence whenever he could. Besides, he'd only live once. He jogged up close enough to be heard, but not so close that she could turn around and slap him; he'd learned that lesson the hard way. "Hey, Pixie!" he called.

Olivia whirled around and met his gaze with more anger in her eyes than he'd thought such a tiny body could hold. "What!?" she spat, and he almost flinched.

"Nothing. I just wanted to see if you're alright," he answered.

She stared at him as if she couldn't believe her ears. "Do I *look* like I'm alright?" she demanded.

"You look like you want to kill somebody," he said, keeping his voice low and calm as if he were dealing with a wild animal. Which, in a way, he was. "Do you maybe want to talk about it first? I'd hate to see a girl like you go to prison."

Olivia scoffed, shoving her hand through her hair like it had wronged her in some way. Sunlight caught the strands as they slipped through her fingers, and Noah decided the color made him think of Cherry Coke—somehow shifting from brown to red as she moved. "What I want is to hurt something," she snarled.

Her words sparked an idea in Noah's mind. "We can do that," he said, thinking on the fly.

Olivia looked at him like he'd grown an extra head. "I was going to eat my feelings at the dessert bar," she replied. "I don't *actually* want to go to prison."

Noah smiled slightly. "Not prison, the arcade," he amended.

"The arcade," she echoed. It wasn't a question.

"Yes. Come with me," Noah said. Taking a risk, he reached for her hand and closed his fingers around hers before she could pro-test. Then he pulled her in the direction he'd been going anyway.

"If we end up in your basement, I will remove your eyeballs with a spoon," Olivia warned as she hurried to keep up with his longer strides.

Noah slowed his pace, though he couldn't help but laugh. "Noted," he said.

"And my older brothers are both marines. They can take your arms off your body and beat you with them," she added, though she hadn't let go of his hand.

"Just trust me, Pixie. No spoons required," he said, and he felt his smile stretch tighter.

Forget Roman candles—this girl was a full-size mortar shell! Good thing they were the best kind.

❧

"YOU ACTUALLY MEANT the arcade," Olivia said skeptically, staring up at the neon letters over the building's front entrance.

"I told you! It's cheaper than therapy and more fun than prison," Noah explained. "Plus, you can win stuff when you're done." He opened the glass door with an exaggerated flourish before following her inside. "Pick your poison: Skee-Ball, air hockey, Whack-A-Mole, or the pièce de résistance—batting cages, five pitches for a dollar."

He watched her look around the dimly lit room, her face painted by the colored lights of two dozen flashing game consoles. A bored-looking teenager slumped behind a long prize counter where glass shelves showcased everything from plastic party poppers to small appliances. Over the boy's head was a full-size kayak and a glittering sign declaring it could be taken home for *only* twelve thousand tickets.

"I want to hit something with a bat," she said firmly, and Noah chuckled.

"Alright. If the lady wants a bat, she gets a bat," he said. He went ahead to the counter, pulled his wallet from his back pocket and put a couple of bills on the smudged glass. "Give me two, Garrett."

The boy surveyed Olivia with obvious surprise before taking the bills and exchanging them for two gold-colored tokens. "Sure thing, man. 'Bout time you brought a chick in with you."

Noah gave a vague sort of grunt, as if that were somehow an answer, and took the tokens from where they lay on the countertop before turning around. "After you, Pix," he said, holding his arm out toward another door on their right.

Olivia went in the direction he pointed. "You come here a lot, I take it?" she asked.

He shrugged as they left the main building and wandered into the outdoor area beyond. To the left was the entrance to an eighteen-hole mini-golf course, and straight ahead was a curvy go-cart track complete with a tunnel. But Noah went to the right, toward a towering wall of chain-link fencing.

"Like I said, it's cheaper than therapy and more fun than prison," he repeated. They passed a rack of helmets, and he grabbed a small black one from the top row. "Here," he said, handing it to her. "You'll want number four. It's got the smoothest pitcher."

Noah went ahead and loaded one of his tokens into the console at cage four. A round "start" button flashed green, and he waited while Olivia chose a bat from the rack and joined him by the fence. She dropped her purse on the ground and then gathered her hair into a low ponytail before securing it with an elastic from around her wrist.

"Alright. You know what you're doing?" he asked.

She put on the helmet. "Yeah."

"Okay, then." He held the gate open as the mechanical pitcher whirred to life. "Have at it."

Olivia stepped up to where home plate was painted on the artificial turf. Noah pressed the button, and there was an audible click as a ball fell into place. She raised the bat to her shoulder and bent her knees. The first pitch flew through the air in a perfect arc, and she swung hard.

"Strike one!" he shouted. He leaned against the fence and hooked his fingers into the chain link above his head. She turned around, and he couldn't help but grin at her obvious annoyance.

"Shut up!" she snapped, and she prepared for another pitch. The second throw followed the first in a beautiful curve, and she swung again. This time she tipped the ball, making contact but sending it behind the plate.

Noah cleared his throat with a strangled noise, trying not to laugh. "It's supposed to go *that way*," he said, pointing toward the far end of the lane. Olivia turned and glowered at him from beneath the brim of her helmet, and he wisely shut his mouth.

She seemed to find her rhythm with the third and fourth pitches, sending them rolling back toward the wall as harmless grounders, and the fifth finally met her bat with a satisfying smack.

Noah watched it fly through the air and bounce off the wall with a thud. "Again?" he asked, already moving toward the console with his second token in hand.

"Again," she confirmed.

She went through another five pitches, hitting all but one with a solid crack, and when the machinery wound down again, she ripped the helmet off her head with new light in her eyes.

Several strands of damp hair clung to her cheeks, which were red with exertion, though somehow that only made her prettier.

"Why haven't I thought of this before?" she said, panting slightly.

"You don't have the same juvenile tendencies that I do," Noah answered.

"Cheaper than therapy and more fun than prison," Olivia echoed as she opened the cage door and walked through. She set her helmet on an overturned bucket, leaned against the fence and sank down until she was sitting on the concrete. Then she tipped her head back against the chain link, soaking up what was probably some of the last warm sunshine of the season.

Noah lowered himself down beside her and stretched his legs out across the sidewalk. "So, Big Brothers Big Sisters, huh?" he asked, nodding toward the logo on her shirt. "Is that for your major?"

"Sort of. I'm in social work, so any work with kids is relevant, but I've been a BBBS volunteer since high school," she answered.

"Why?"

Olivia turned to look at him with a curious expression. "Why not?" she asked. "There are so many kids in the world who just need somebody to show up—somebody to cheer them on from the sidelines, listen when they need to talk, push them on the swings. If I can be that person, even once or twice a week, then I want to do it."

Something warm surged through Noah's veins. "So, you're Super Pixie?"

She ducked her head with a soft smile, and Noah felt like he'd done something incredible. "Maybe," she said. Then her face fell, and she let out a long, tired sigh. "But some kids have more problems than just listening can fix."

Noah looked across the lawn where it stretched toward the arcade. A father and his young son had just exited the main building, and their matching orange T-ball shirts seemed to glow in the afternoon sun. A pang of longing pierced Noah's chest as a memory flashed through his mind, and he could almost feel the impact of a baseball in the palm of his hand as he and his own father threw it back and forth in a weekend tradition that had lasted for years. Until, one day, it was over—that old glove discarded beside all the other things his dad had left behind.

"You'd be surprised what just showing up can do, Pix," he said. "You can't control what they go through at home, but you can make sure they always have someone in their corner." He paused to clear his throat, pushing the words past a knot in his chest. "Just being around will do more than you'll ever realize," he finished.

Olivia didn't answer for a moment. Finally, she gave a small smile and bumped her shoulder against his. "You know, there might be hope for you yet, Campbell," she said. Then she seemed to pause and think for a moment. "Do you drink soda?"

He frowned, confused by the topic shift. "Umm, yeah. Doesn't everyone?"

"Can you start keeping your can tabs? And maybe ask your friends, too? I need a whole bunch of them, like, a whole, *whole* bunch."

He cocked his head. "Is this about a kid?" he asked, trying to piece the puzzle together.

"Yeah. And an owl and an art project."

"Got it," he replied, though he wasn't totally sure he did. "Yeah, I can keep the tabs," he agreed. Then a perfect segue popped into his mind. "So if I'm collecting can tabs for you . . . does that mean I can have your number?"

She turned sharply and leveled him with a serious stare, though humor still danced behind her eyes. "I'm not going out with you," she said firmly.

Noah felt his eyebrows go up. "Well, that's irrelevant since I didn't ask you out."

"But you're going to."

"Oh-ho!" he crowed. "Somebody thinks an awful lot of herself, doesn't she?"

Olivia snorted and leaned back against the fence. "I'm just saying. I'm not going out with you."

"Okay. Now, your number, please?" He pulled his cell phone from his pocket and typed in the digits as Olivia rattled them off. Then he sent her a text message, just to be sure.

Her purse vibrated by her side, and she fished through it before pulling out her own phone. Then she read the message aloud. "'Noah Campbell—grocery thief, snake wrangler, couch delivery person.' Really?"

Noah shrugged and smiled up at the sky. "Just in case you forget," he replied.

She huffed, and he cut his eyes over to find her typing out a message of her own. His phone buzzed seconds later, and he raised it to eye level. "'Olivia Cohen—yard sale princess, popcorn hoarder, not going out with you.'" He laughed as the last words left his lips.

"Just in case you forget," she echoed smugly, and Noah lolled his head against the chain link.

"Oh, trust me, Pixie. I won't."

4

NOAH: I'm afraid one of my customers is going to leave me 17 cats.

OLIVIA: 17 cats? As in...

NOAH: As in 17 cats. In her will. When she dies.

NOAH: Probably because they killed her.

OLIVIA: Why?

NOAH: Beats me, but she talks about them as if I'm going to meet them soon. Today she said little Tiger will love me because we have the same color eyes.

NOAH: What am I going to do with 17 cats?

OLIVIA: Anything but bring them to my house. I've got enough to deal with.

NOAH: Like what? What could you possibly have to do that you're too busy to help me sack up ten pounds of cat poop every day?

OLIVIA: Well, I was stupid and gave a super annoying guy my number, for one. He never stops talking.

NOAH: Why don't you just tell him to shut up?

OLIVIA: Shut up.

NOAH: Yeah, that's not going to work. Nice try though.

TUESDAY, NOVEMBER 8

NOAH: I know what you said, but are you sure you won't go out with me?

> **OLIVIA:** Yes. I'm sure.

> **NOAH:** Because I'm intimidating?

> **OLIVIA:** As if!

> **OLIVIA:** I could take you in a heartbeat.

> **NOAH:** Ha! Dream on, sister.

> **OLIVIA:** I'm not your sister.

> **NOAH:** Thank heaven for that.

"WHO IS THAT smile for?" Lexie asked, a knowing look on her face as she came back into her room that Friday night.

Olivia quickly shoved her phone underneath her thigh. "Mind your own business," she said, though it was without heat.

Lexie crossed to her dresser and opened the top drawer before pulling out a soft blue sweater and a tank top. "Have you told him about the Harrelson Center?"

"Told who?" Olivia asked innocently.

Lexie met her friend's eyes in her vanity mirror, clearly seeing through the act. "The guy blowing up your phone at all hours of the night. Every night. For a week," she replied.

Olivia's phone chose that moment to buzz loudly against her leg, and she swallowed a sigh. There wasn't any point trying to downplay the number of times Noah texted her each day.

Anything less than twenty would be a lie, and at least one of those was always an attempt to change her mind. "It's not my fault he doesn't have an off button," she grumbled.

Lexie only laughed softly. "You've never had a problem telling boys to get lost before," she observed, and she added a pair of jeans to the growing pile of clothing on her bed.

Olivia pursed her lips and picked at a loose thread on Lexie's comforter. Her friend was right; she'd never had an issue telling guys to leave her alone—unwanted attention was an unfortunate side effect of good genes, and she'd learned to be proactive about it over the years. And yet, as persistent as Noah was, she simply hadn't found the right time to send him packing.

"I just think he might be interested to know you're going to be interning down the street from the grocery store where he works," Lexie went on, ignoring her friend's silence.

"Maybe that's why I haven't told him," Olivia replied. "He doesn't need another way to drive me nuts." Her phone buzzed again, and Lexie smiled.

"Is he driving you nuts? Could have fooled me," she murmured, and she shut her last dresser drawer with a bang. "Alright, I think that's everything," she added.

"Everything for what?"

"My mystery date!" Lexie answered.

Olivia looked at the pile of items her friend had selected. "For when?" she asked, confused. The clock on Lexie's bedside table said it was almost 11:00 p.m.

"For tonight. Jake's created some kind of all-night surprise for our one-month anniversary, and he said to wear extra layers," Lexie explained. She picked up her phone from the nightstand and unlocked it before turning the screen toward Olivia.

"Extra layers?" Olivia asked skeptically, reading from the text message. "What kind of romantic all-nighter requires extra layers?"

Lexie shrugged and put the phone down before pulling on a pair of jeans over fleece-lined leggings. "No idea. I've tried to get it out of him, but he's holding this pretty close to the vest. The only thing that makes sense is if we'll be outside."

"Outside?" Olivia blurted. "It's November!"

"Which is why winter layers would make sense," Lexie answered, sliding the sweater over her head.

Olivia's phone buzzed a third time. Her fingers itched with the need to check it, but she clasped them in her lap instead. She didn't need to give Lexie any more ammunition.

A few minutes later, there was a knock at the front door as Lexie finished brushing her long hair into a ponytail. "That'll be Jake," she said, her voice already full of excitement. "Don't wait up."

"Oh, I won't," Olivia called as her friend walked away. "I'm going to bed and will be sleeping like a baby."

"Check your messages first!" Lexie shouted back, and Olivia rolled her eyes. She'd check her messages when she was good and ready.

But, as it turned out, Noah was impatient as well as persistent. Her phone started to vibrate in a relentless staccato almost the moment the front door shut behind her friend—a phone call this time, not just a text.

"Has it ever occurred to you that I might be busy?" she asked the moment the line connected.

"Is Jexie still there?"

Olivia blinked, startled by the unexpectedly strange question. "Is what?" she asked.

"Is Jexie still there?" Noah repeated, slower this time. "You know, Jake and Lexie?"

Comprehension dawned, and Olivia felt her face wrinkle in disgust. "Jexie? Seriously?"

"Yeah, isn't that what we do these days? We smash people's names together when they start dating?"

"Ugh, please don't," she groaned. "They're still two separate people."

"Are you sure about that? The other day, I caught them eating from the same sandwich," he replied, and Olivia chuckled without meaning to.

"Okay, that is kind of gross," she conceded. "But honestly, I'm just glad she's happy." She pushed off Lexie's bed and padded down the hall to the kitchen. Then she opened one of the upper cabinets and pulled down a box of popcorn. She turned it upside down and frowned when only one plastic-wrapped bag fell onto the countertop. "So, do you know where they're going?" she asked.

"Of course I do! You know, being the best friend and all," he answered.

Olivia rolled her eyes. She could almost hear him preening. She tilted her head and clamped the phone between her ear and shoulder while she used both hands to free her snack from its package. "Uh-huh. So, what's the big surprise, Mr. Best Friend?"

"Oh, I can't tell you that," he said quickly. "I've been sworn to secrecy—crossed my heart and everything."

Olivia huffed as she yanked open the microwave door and stuffed the folded bag inside. Then she shut the door and entered the perfect cook time; no true connoisseur ever used the "popcorn" button. "They're already gone, genius," she shot back. "How am I going to ruin the surprise now?"

The line went silent as he apparently thought this over. "Fair point," he conceded. "In that case, he's taking her out to the middle of nowhere to watch tonight's meteor shower from the back of his truck, complete with picnic basket and extra blankets. Totally making every other man on the planet look bad."

There was a teasing note to his voice, but Olivia got the impression he was secretly impressed by his friend's ingenuity. *She* certainly was! Lexie was going to be bursting at the seams by the time she got home.

But that wasn't the detail Olivia chose to dwell on just then. "Wow! You caved *so fast!*" she taunted. "I'm gonna have to tell Jake to revoke your security clearance."

"Wait, wha—"

"Crumpled like a house of cards!" she went on, raising her voice to be heard above the increasingly loud pops of the microwave. "I didn't even have to beg! Some secret keeper you are." She grinned, glad he couldn't see her.

"Wha . . . Okay, first of all, that wasn't fair," he stammered.

Olivia couldn't help but laugh at the tone of his voice.

"And secondly, I am an *excellent* secret keeper! You have no idea the kinds of gems I'm hiding in this brain of mine. I am a *vault!*" he insisted.

The sounds of exploding corn kernels began to slow, and Olivia pulled open the microwave door once they stopped. She waved her hand in front of the appliance, trying to dissipate some of the steam that burst from the opening. "A vault, huh?"

"Yes. Once something goes in here, it does *not* come back out!"

"With some obvious exceptions, though, right?" Olivia teased.

"Shut up."

"Hey! Gentlemen do not tell ladies to shut up," she pointed out, and Noah made a sarcastic sort of noise.

"Ladies don't trick gentlemen out of classified information," he grumbled.

She carried her snack down the hall to her own room, then she sat on the bed and crossed her legs beneath herself. She knew she shouldn't encourage him like this, but he was just so much fun to mess with.

"Hey, what are the chances you want to come watch this meteor shower with me, since you're awake anyway?" he asked. "Our backyard is pretty dark; no streetlights or anything. I've seen a few already."

Olivia sorted through her bag of popcorn, searching for a kernel with the perfect butter-to-corn ratio, while she briefly imagined sharing a warm blanket with Noah under the stars. The offer was tempting—more tempting than she wanted to admit . . . which automatically made it a bad idea.

"Come on, Pix. I don't bite," he added after a moment. "Well, not hard, anyway. And not without permission."

Olivia huffed and pulled a fleece blanket across her lap, as if that would weigh her down. "Give up, Campbell," she said. "I'm already in my pajamas. I'm not changing again for you."

"Well, then don't!" he protested. "Pajamas are always welcome here. Besides, I've got a bag of can tabs for you to pick up."

She shook her head and rolled her eyes toward the ceiling. "I'll get them later. Just watch your stars," she warned, though she couldn't keep the humor out of her voice. "I've got an early morning anyway, so I should probably go to bed."

"Bummer! Well, goodnight then, Pixie," he answered.

But then, nothing happened.

Olivia glanced at her screen to make sure the call timer had stopped.

It hadn't.

"Campbell?"

"Yeah?"

"Hang up!"

"No, you hang up!"

"No, you— Agh! You know what, I'm not twelve, so goodnight."

She could hear him laughing even as she pulled the phone from her ear and pressed the red "end call" button. She snuggled down beneath her blanket and reached for the television remote with no real intention of going to sleep.

Minutes later, her phone vibrated again.

NOAH: Just saw one. Wished you were here. Then a bird pooped on my head.

Olivia laughed out loud, the sound echoing back to her in the empty apartment.

Serves him right!

5

NOAH WASHED HIS hands for the sixth time, scrubbing at the blue stains on his palms and fingers. Then he glanced into the chipped bathroom mirror. His ears and neck were also blue, as was his hair—though it was less noticeable than if he'd been blond. He had to hand it to Conner, though; it was a respectable effort.

Finally turning off the water, he yanked his phone from his pocket and called the first person he could think of who might have the experience he needed. "Hey," he said when she answered. "How would you wash the red out of your hair?"

"I wouldn't. I paid a lot of money to look this good," Olivia said.

Noah huffed at his reflection. "Okay, well, I didn't, so help a guy out."

There was a long pause, and he could almost feel her confusion.

"I'm missing something here. Did you dye your hair?"

"Not intentionally, no," he mumbled, massaging his fingertips against the bridge of his nose. He instantly thought better of it and yanked them away before searching his reflection for any signs that the color had transferred to his face. Thankfully, it hadn't.

Olivia snorted in a decidedly unladylike way. "Oh, I've got to see this!" she crowed. "What is it? Orange? Purple?"

"Just tell me how to wash it out!" he groaned, though her audible glee made an involuntary smile inch across his face. "And how to get it off my skin."

"Do you look like an Oompa-Loompa? *Please* tell me you look like an Oompa-Loompa!"

"Pixie . . ."

"Okay, okay! I've got an idea, but I'll make you a deal. Jexie has set up camp in my living room, and I'd rather not be here if I can help it," she said, and Noah clamped his lips together to hold back a laugh.

"I thought we weren't calling them that," he reminded her, and Olivia sighed.

"Look, do you want my help or not? You give me someplace to hang out, and I'll do my best to return you to your normal color."

Noah looked around the small bathroom he shared with Conner, noting the towels hanging on every possible surface and the clothes piling up in the corners. The rest of the house wasn't much better; even the air held the distinct smell of too many young men in one place.

"Alright, fine, but don't expect the Taj Mahal," he said, relenting. He didn't see that he had much choice; his hair he could probably live with, but the only way to see the back of his neck was to hold a smaller mirror in one hand, and it would be a lot easier to fix if he had help.

He could almost hear Olivia roll her eyes. "Give me thirty minutes," she said, and then the line went dead.

Noah gathered the laundry from the bathroom and dumped it into his hamper. Then he wandered across the hall into the kitchen. He eyed the orange paint splatters on the once cream-colored walls—courtesy of the indoor paintball ambush he'd staged earlier in the semester. The green-and-white linoleum was scuffed and dirty, peeling along the baseboards. Some of the cabinet doors hung crooked, and the thick carpet in the adjoining living room was the same dingy brown as the sagging couch along one wood-paneled wall. It was a good thing Conner's dad was planning to tear the place down after they graduated; it really wasn't fit for human habitation.

He sighed, running his hand through his tinted hair. There wasn't much he could do about any of that right now. The house was what it was, and what it *was* was a dilapidated bachelor pad. He sent Olivia a text with the address and made his way to the kitchen sink before lifting the first of a large pile of crusty dishes from its resting place.

If he only had half an hour, he'd better get to work.

❧

A KNOCK ON the front door interrupted Noah's chaotic attempt to separate clean clothes from their already-worn counterparts and prompted him to shove the entire pile into his bedroom closet and shut the door.

The knock came again, faster this time.

"I'm coming!" he called, tripping over somebody's discarded backpack on his way through the living room. Probably Conner's.

The seldom-used dead bolt on the front door screeched when he unlocked it.

"Why didn't you just come through the garage?" he asked, stepping out of the way as Olivia breezed inside.

"Oh, is that what you call that part over there?" she said, jerking her chin toward the far end of the house. "It looks more like the kind of shed where serial killers hang the bodies." She dumped two boxes of pizza and a Walmart bag onto the kitchen table and turned to look at him, her hands on her hips. "Well? Let me see," she ordered, beckoning him forward with a curl of her fingers.

Noah paused, having almost forgotten why he'd called her. His hand flew self-consciously to his head, but Olivia reached up and pulled his wrist away. Her other hand combed through his hair as she surveyed the damage.

Electricity seemed to arc from her fingertips across his scalp, and it was all he could do not to lean against her hand like a cat. As it was, he had to tell himself to stand still as she moved slowly around him, first rubbing a lock of his hair between her fingers, then grazing her thumbs along the back of his neck and ears. Every cell in his body was on high alert by the time she'd made a full circuit.

"I'm gonna guess color-depositing conditioner of some kind," she finally said, breaking the silence. She reached for his hands and turned them until they were both palm up. "You're supposed to wear gloves."

"Well, thankfully, I noticed the color before I washed the rest of my body with it."

"You wash your skin with shampoo?"

"I'm out of body wash," he answered matter-of-factly.

She wrinkled her nose as if that weren't a perfectly acceptable answer. Then, she turned and made her way back to the table, where the things she'd brought still waited.

"You didn't have to bring food," he observed, though his stomach growled in disagreement. He stepped up beside her and opened the top box of pizza before removing a slice of sausage-and-pepperoni. He folded it in half and then devoured it.

Olivia ignored him and continued sorting the contents of the plastic sack. "I know, but Jake had just started *Ghostbusters*, and I'm really grateful for someplace else to be—even if it is with you."

"Oh, ha, ha," he said dryly as he reached for another slice. "I'm glad my predicament was useful for you."

"The timing was convenient, yes," she replied. She held up a bottle of blue Dawn soap, and Noah narrowed his eyes skeptically.

"Dish soap? That's your big idea? You could have told me that over the phone," he said between bites.

"Yeah, but this way I get to see the problem for myself," she replied. She was grinning from ear to ear.

"You think it'll work?"

Olivia raised both shoulders before looking down at the bottle and pointing to a picture on the front. "It washes crude oil off these adorable baby ducks, so surely there's hope for you," she said, her eyes flashing with humor. "Now, go scrub."

He took the bottle and started back toward the hall. "What, you're not going to help?" he asked when she didn't follow.

She rolled her eyes, but a smile gave her amusement away. "As much as I'd love a chance to waterboard you, I think I'll pass," she said. She reached for the pizza box and lifted a slice with one hand. "Now, hurry, or I'll eat the rest of this myself."

Noah heeded her warning and went to shower, collecting new clothes from his dresser on the way. Two shampoos later, he emerged to find Olivia waiting for him in the kitchen, surrounded by a makeshift salon of her own creation.

"Sit here and lean forward," she said, pointing to a chair she'd turned backwards beside the table. He threw one leg over it and crossed his arms along the back rail before resting his forehead on top of them. Olivia assessed his hair again, this time moving more slowly than she had before.

Noah found his eyes drifting closed.

"The dish soap should help open your follicles and release the excess color, but it'll still take at least a week. You're lucky you aren't blond; you'd look like a blueberry lollipop," she said. "The staining on your skin is going to take some scrubbing, though." She brushed her hands over his neck again and tipped his ears forward to check behind them. Then she tugged the neckline of his shirt back, as if she were peeking between his shoulder blades.

"I can take that off if you want," he murmured, and she smacked the back of his head in a playful way.

"I'm just checking the damage!" she insisted, and Noah grinned, though he knew she couldn't see his face. He wished he could peek back to see hers; maybe he'd finally gotten her to blush.

Her hands moved away, and Noah heard her step closer to the table. He opened his eyes and looked down at her socks, which were red and had little pom-pom things around the ankles. He didn't remember seeing her take off the boots she'd been wearing when she came in, but he was glad she'd decided to make herself at home without asking. There was something about that that he liked—a lot.

Noah raised his head and eyed the supplies she'd laid out on the tabletop: rubbing alcohol, Q-tips and a bag of fluffy cotton balls. She pressed a piece of white fluff to the top of the alcohol bottle and tipped the whole thing over and back in one quick motion.

"This will be cold," she cautioned.

Noah put his forehead back down on his arms. "I can handle it," he said, but he flinched when she pressed the cotton ball to the nape of his neck.

Olivia chuckled before scrubbing the soft material along his hairline. "I thought you could handle it."

"Well, yeah, but you've had that in the freezer!" he declared.

"Just my car, and only for the drive over," she countered. "Now stop whining and be a man about it!"

Noah grumbled quietly, though not with any real irritation. He liked the way she always gave as good as she got; it kept things interesting.

They both lapsed into silence as she worked the cotton ball in tight circles across the back of his neck, replenishing the alcohol periodically. He waited for the quiet to start crawling up his spine like ants, the way it always did when no one had anything to say, but the sensation never came. Instead, it felt comfortable—familiar, even. It was a phenomenon he couldn't explain.

While she wasn't being particularly gentle, there was something about the pressure against his neck that was oddly soothing. Noah felt the muscles in his shoulders gradually uncoil as the minutes stretched on, and finally, a long breath escaped from his chest.

Olivia chuckled. "Well, who knew?"

"Who knew what?" Noah mumbled.

"Who knew the best way to find your off button was to dye you an unnatural color? I would have tried this weeks ago." She laughed. "By the way, you're normal all the way to here." She ran her fingertip in a horizontal line halfway down the left side of his neck.

Trapezius muscle, his brain automatically filled in. It was apparently still working even as the rest of his body was being lulled into a coma. He grunted in acknowledgement, content to let her work her magic for as long as she wanted. He let his head loll to one side and cracked his eyes open, hoping he might be able to see her over his shoulder, but he couldn't.

Olivia kept working until she was apparently satisfied with the results, at which point she dropped her last cotton ball onto a growing pile on the table. It landed with a damp thud. "All done, I think," she said, and she gave the tops of his shoulders a quick squeeze. "You can work on your hands yourself."

He groaned again and pushed up to a sitting position, surprised to find he wasn't tense from being half slumped against the chair rail for so long. He rolled his head in a circle and stretched his arms toward the ceiling. Then he stopped and watched as Olivia packed her supplies—though she left the alcohol behind for him.

"Don't you ever think these practical jokes are a bit childish?" she asked after a minute or so.

"Oh, all the time," he answered truthfully. "But the way I see it, I'm gonna have to be an adult forever. I've got plenty of time to make good choices and use my prefrontal cortex to its full capacity, but right now I can still have some fun and get away with it . . . so why not? I'll be a grown-up when I'm thirty."

"Thirty, huh? Is that when boys finally become men?"

"Give or take a decade. My mom's brother is forty-two, and he still draws body parts on dirty car windshields, so it's not guaranteed."

Olivia laughed and turned around, leaning on the counter with the heels of her hands. "Do you know how you're going to get Conner back?" she asked.

"Not yet," he admitted. "But I'm open to suggestions."

Olivia pulled her bottom lip between her teeth and worried it in a way Noah found incredibly distracting. He momentarily lost his train of thought, instead following a completely different set of tracks that ended with him pinning her in place against the cabinetry.

"I have an idea," she said, "but it would have to wait until tomorrow."

It took Noah a few seconds to get back to the topic at hand, and he blinked several times to clear his mind. When he did, the only word he really retained was "tomorrow," and it suddenly didn't matter what the idea was. "Fabulous, it's a date!" he declared.

Olivia raised one eyebrow and crossed her arms over her chest defiantly. "No, not a date," she corrected. "I am not going out with you, remember?"

"You're going somewhere, and you're coming with me, right? So, technically, you *are* going out with me," he said with a wolfish grin, and Olivia narrowed her eyes.

"Yes, we would be going somewhere, but Campbell, repeat after me: This is not a date," she said slowly.

"La la la la, I can't hear you!" he sang, clapping his hands over his ears. He headed toward the living room, and he could feel her hot on his heels.

"Campbell!" she shouted, but he only smiled and sang even louder as he made a circuit around the coffee table. He was going to make the most of this chance, even if it killed him.

Which, judging by the look on her face, it might.

ON SATURDAY AFTERNOON, Olivia pulled her Mustang into Noah's driveway, which was more mud than gravel, and honked her horn twice.

He came out through the garage and half jogged to her car. "Don't you know you're not supposed to honk when you pick up a date?" he asked as he opened the passenger's side door and slid inside.

She turned in her seat and pinned him with the kind of look she usually reserved for her brothers. "Campbell, this is not a date," she said again, even though she knew the effort was futile. He still hadn't said those words back to her, despite several days of pressing on her part.

"You're also supposed to open the door for me," he added, shaking his head as if truly disappointed. "I really thought you'd be better at this."

Olivia bit the inside of her cheek to keep her amusement in check. Why was he always making her laugh? If she had a brain in her head, she'd still be curled up on her couch watching *Friends* reruns.

But apparently, her common sense was on vacation.

"This is a revenge excursion only. There is no version of a date where I go shopping for creepy dolls," she replied.

Noah rubbed his hands together quickly, and his face split into an evil sort of grin. "I hope we find one that's haunted," he said, apparently ignoring the rest of her statement.

She pursed her lips and chose not to belabor the point.

"So, where are we going, anyway?" he asked.

She backed out of the driveway and started toward the nearby town of Willow Creek. "You'll see," she answered mysteriously.

"Oh, surprise location!" he blurted. "Okay, points for that, Pix."

Olivia sighed deeply and kept her eyes on the road. A little while later, she pulled into the empty parking lot of a building that looked as if it had been accidentally dropped onto the pavement, like Dorothy's house in *The Wizard of Oz*. A creaking sign above the front door read "Beulah Mae's Bargain Boutique."

Noah was the first one out of the car, and he stood looking up at the structure with one hand shielding his eyes. "I'm not sure 'boutique' is the word they were looking for," he said, and Olivia chuckled as she rounded the front of the car.

"Oh, come on, Campbell! I've wanted to stop here for ages, but no one ever wants to come with me."

"There might be a reason for that," he said dryly, but he followed anyway as she approached the door. A bell tinkled above her head as they passed inside, and all sound seemed to cease when the door closed behind them. Even their footsteps seemed to be muffled.

Olivia looked around. They weren't in any sort of store she'd ever seen before, but rather at the entrance of what seemed to be an unending maze of shelves, crates and racks of all shapes and sizes. Every surface was covered in . . . well . . . *stuff*. Typewriters and frilly hats, china plates and glass lighthouses, carved wooden pepper shakers and costume jewelry—you name it, it was there. Olivia felt the low hum of excitement building inside her chest. This was like an estate sale on steroids.

"Yep. Anything we find in here is *definitely* haunted," Noah said from behind her.

She turned sharply and smacked his chest with the back of her hand, but any response he may have had was cut off by the hacking cough of someone nearby. Olivia and Noah both jumped and peered around a dressmaker's mannequin to find an ancient-looking woman standing behind a rolltop desk.

"Welcome to Beulah Mae's Bargain Boutique," she said kindly, though her voice sounded as if she hadn't used it in a very long time. "Browse at your leisure, and please let me know if you need anything. There are bells on the walls at regular intervals if you get lost."

If they got lost?! Well, that wasn't ominous at all.

Olivia glanced back at Noah, who seemed to be fighting a smile. "Thank you!" she told the shopkeeper, and she waved to the woman before turning down the first narrow walkway to their right. It was lined on both sides with low tables covered in beaded handbags.

"Points deducted for potential to die," Noah whispered.

She shushed him with a quick wave of her hand. "She'll hear you!" she admonished quietly. "Besides, this is not a date, and I'm not being graded."

Noah made an amused sort of noise but didn't answer one way or the other.

They moved through the aisles in silence for some time, occasionally stopping to examine an item more closely. Eventually, they wove their way through the main room and down a short flight of stairs. Olivia stopped abruptly at the bottom, and Noah bumped into her from behind.

"Which way?" she asked, peering down each of four walkways in turn. She almost felt like they should be leaving a trail of breadcrumbs, just in case.

Noah leaned around her and examined their options. "This way," he announced, as if he actually knew where they were going. He stepped past her and started down a narrow trail to the right, and Olivia followed. She scanned the shelves and tables as they went, though she didn't see any of the white-faced porcelain dolls they'd come for.

"Let's look in here," she said, turning into an alcove on their left. The low shelves were filled with children's toys from years past—plastic rotary phones, stiff-legged army men and carved wooden animals. Finally, in the back behind a faded teddy bear, Olivia saw it: a brightly painted smile. "I found one!" she crowed, more excited than she'd expected to be. It was like stumbling across the proverbial needle in the haystack.

She reached past a few cobwebs and retrieved the doll. Its unnaturally blue eyes did in fact seem to follow her as she turned it from side to side, and its whole body needed a good cleaning, but since its only current purpose was to freak Conner out, it was perfect. "Hey, do you see any more?" she asked. She turned around but was surprised to find herself alone. "Campbell?" she called loudly. "Where'd you go?"

"Where'd *you* go?" asked a muffled voice. It was somewhere off to the left, but when Olivia poked her head back into the main walkway, she saw there was more than one branch stretching off in that direction.

She tucked the doll under one arm and cupped both hands around her mouth. "Marco!" she yelled.

"Polo!"

She stepped carefully along the hall and peered into each little nook as she passed. "Marco!" she shouted again.

"Polo!" came a second response, but now it seemed to be behind her.

"Stop moving!" she ordered.

"*You* stop moving!"

Olivia huffed out an agitated breath. They could play this game for months and never find each other. "Campbell, I will leave you in here if I have to!" she threatened. She started walking toward where she'd last heard his voice, retracing her steps down the hall and making another turn. But it seemed like the dust itself had absorbed all the ambient sound. She stopped and listened hard, straining to pick up any footsteps in her vicinity. There was nothing.

"Campbell?" she shouted.

No answer.

The eerie silence made the hairs on the back of her neck stand up of their own accord. "Noah?" she called again, though it came out softer this time. Maybe he'd been swallowed up by a wardrobe or something equally outrageous.

Then, there was a sound. A quiet sort of thud that she couldn't attribute to anything in particular. She turned on the spot and peered down the dimly lit aisleway behind her, but it was empty.

"No—AH!" She screamed the last syllable as something grabbed her from behind. The doll she'd been holding hit the floor and rolled several feet away, and whatever had attacked her started to cackle. "Noah Campbell, I hate you!" she yelled, turning as the arms released her.

He doubled over, bracing one hand on a low table as he laughed. When he straightened again, she could see the shine of moisture in his eyes. "That was perfect!" he wheezed. "When you turned around . . ."

"You're an idiot," she grumbled, and she pressed one hand against where her heart was running wild inside her chest. "I found what we needed, by the way. Now we can look for a way out." She turned to retrieve the doll where it lay on the floor but paused when Noah's warm hand closed around her wrist.

"Umm, no, you mean *I* can look for the way out. *You're* staying right here," he said. Then, in the time it took Olivia to turn her head, something hard and cold joined his fingers—and clicked.

She looked down at the silver bracelet in shock. Her eyes

found the short chain on one side before following it to a second bracelet, which Noah still held in his hand. Before she could process what was happening, he'd latched the metal ring onto a heavy clothing rack. Then he flashed her a blinding grin.

Olivia yanked on her arm and watched as the chain on the handcuffs snapped taut, stopping her movement in midair. She felt her mouth fall open. "Where did you get this?"

"Over there." He gestured along the hall in the direction she'd been going.

"You found the keys, too, right?" she demanded, shaking her wrist inside the bracelet.

Noah scoffed and crouched to grab the doll, which thankfully didn't seem to be broken. "*Of course* I found the keys! I do have a brain, you know."

"Okay, then take it off," she ordered.

He stood and stubbornly shook his head. "No."

"No? What do you mean *no*?!"

"I mean no. You're the one who got lost, and then you threatened to leave me behind! This feels like appropriate punishment."

"Appropriate pun—"

"And," he went on, raising his voice to talk over her, "you haven't told me I look pretty tonight or anything! Terrible date behavior. I believe you owe me an apology." He stuck his bottom lip out in an exaggerated pout.

Olivia gaped, torn between laughing and trying to hit him. "This is not a date!" she said instead, blurting out the only thing that came to mind.

"Okay, well, in that case, it won't be bad form for me to leave you here," he said, and he turned on his heel and started down the gloomy corridor.

Olivia waited for him to turn around, waited for the punch line to come, but then he turned a corner at the end of the aisle and disappeared from sight. She groaned and rubbed her free hand across her forehead. "Campbell," she called, hardly believing she was giving in. "I'm sorry I said I'd leave you."

A few seconds passed, and then she dimly saw the outline of his head and shoulders pop from beyond a bookshelf. "Is that all?" he asked.

Olivia rolled her lips together and tried not to smile. "And you look pretty tonight!" she shouted. "Now get back here and turn me loose!"

The rest of Noah's body appeared in her line of sight, and he sauntered back to where she stood. He put the doll on a table before crossing his arms over his chest in a pose that made his muscles more prominent, even in the half-light. "Turn you loose, huh?" he drawled. He took another step, and his eyes sparkled with the kind of mischief that could get a girl into a lot of trouble.

Olivia nodded, refusing to back away as he moved even closer. He held her gaze without speaking, and she felt one warm hand slide down her arm and close around her bound wrist. Then he gently moved it behind her. Her confusion was immediately remedied when he held his free hand up and shook it, rattling the single, silver key that hung from a tiny ring.

Of course he would choose the most difficult way possible to do as she'd asked.

The hand holding the key settled on the curve of her waist before gliding back to join the first at the small of her back. His attention darted down toward her mouth, now only inches from his as he leaned closer.

"Don't kiss me," she warned, though the words were much softer than she'd intended. Something about his proximity made it hard to breathe.

"I wouldn't dream of it, Pix," he murmured, but the way his eyes darkened from gray to denim gave him away. He was, in fact, dreaming of it at that very moment, and Olivia struggled to remember why it was a bad idea.

Try as she might, all she could process was him: the unfairly long lashes that ringed his eyes, the afternoon stubble along the line of his jaw, the way his body heat radiated through the front of her sweater. For a second, he seemed to breathe her in, and then she felt his hands begin to move behind her—first spinning the handcuff around her wrist and then tracing the metal circle until he found the keyhole. Seconds later, there was a faint click, and the bracelet came free.

"Besides," he said, his voice now impossibly breezy, "I don't kiss on the first date." All at once, he stepped away as if nothing at all had just passed between them, and Olivia felt every inch as an unexpected loss.

Her brain screeched to a halt before speeding up again, as if fast-forwarding to their current moment. "What?" she asked.

Noah bit his lip and looked down at her, and the impish look in his eyes said he knew *exactly* what he'd done. "I don't kiss on the first date," he repeated. "What kind of guy do you think I am?"

Olivia realized her mouth was half open, and she shut it with a snap. Her cheeks grew hot in a rare flush, and the delight on Noah's face was obvious.

"You seem upset, Pix!" he crowed, doing a horrible job of concealing his glee—if he was even trying. "Have you changed your mind?" Then he picked up the porcelain doll and started walking away without waiting for an answer.

Olivia took a deep breath and willed her heart to slow down. There was *no way* she'd admit what she was really thinking, which actually wasn't words at all but one long disappointed sound.

Disappointed?!

No. Absolutely not. *Indignant* was more like it. Who did he think he was?

"No, I have not changed my mind!" she spluttered at last, finally putting her feet into motion. "The answer is, and always will be, no!" She caught up with him at the end of the hall, and he turned to face her again.

"Not even one? Just to get it out of your system?" he asked.

"You aren't *in* my system! You aren't even my type!"

His quirked eyebrow only infuriated her further.

"You're *not*!" she insisted.

Humor danced behind his eyes, and he stared down at her without speaking. Then, finally, he shrugged. "Alright."

His sudden change of tune knocked Olivia a little off-balance. "Alright?" she repeated.

"Yeah. Tell yourself whatever you need to, Pix; I know denial when I see it."

Olivia let out a huff that was almost a growl before pushing past him, leading the way back in the only direction that made any sense.

The sooner they found their way out of there, the better.

6

W ATSON'S GROCERY STORE closed at 1:00 p.m. on Thanksgiving Day, and Noah was moving carefully through the traffic of downtown Hampton by 2:30 p.m. It was only an hour south of Cypress Valley, but his hometown often felt like another world entirely. The rolling fields of corn and soybeans that were so prevalent in northwest Tennessee were replaced by multistory office buildings and the tall cranes that unloaded shipping boats along the Mississippi River.

He turned down one side street and then another before finding himself in front of a red-brick apartment complex that had seen better days. He wasn't sure when exactly those days had been, but they were certainly before he and his mother had moved in eight years ago. He parked along the street and climbed from his car, which creaked and groaned with every movement.

The ancient Toyota Camry was just lucky to have made the trip in one piece. Well, in the same number of pieces in which it had left his house that morning, anyway. The rear door handles were missing, replaced by zip ties that only functioned from the outside. The passenger's side window would roll down with ease, but it took three people to put it back up—one pushing from the inside, one pressing from the outside and another holding down the button. Both the bumper and the fender were dented, and the driver's side door hung crooked, only latching if you pulled up on the frame while you closed it.

He didn't bother to lock it when he walked away; not even the thieves in this neighborhood wanted a car like his, and there wasn't anything inside worth stealing.

The sounds of a party met him on the sidewalk, drawing him down the central walkway between buildings three and four. He rounded a corner to the rear patio and found chaos in progress . . . but the good kind.

Doors were open on both sides of the shared outdoor space, and his mother's neighbors scurried in and out, covering long folding tables with mismatched tablecloths, dragging chairs of all kinds out onto the concrete slab, and trying to corral the children who darted around the legs of their elders.

Noah bent down and caught a little girl as she rushed past. "Argh!" he yelled, tossing her into the air.

"Noah!" she squealed. She threw her arms around his neck and held on, already knowing what would come next.

Noah let go of her waist, and she wrapped her short legs around his torso, hanging on like a monkey. She giggled as he shook from side to side. "Get off!" he yelped, spinning around in a half-hearted attempt to dislodge her. His efforts attracted the attention of the others, and soon he was covered in child-sized barnacles. They clung to both his legs, climbed up his sides and leapt onto his back as if conquering Mount Everest.

"Help!" he called at last, conceding the defeat the young ones craved, and a woman nearby laughed fondly.

"It's good to see you, Noah," she called. "Children, let him go."

Noah's captors reluctantly obeyed.

"How long will you be here?"

"Did you bring us candy?"

"My mama's making pie!"

Their excited chatter became a whirlwind of noise, and Noah knelt in the center of the storm. "Just for today, not this time, and that sounds amazing!" he said, answering them each in turn. "But right now I need to see *my* mama. Do you know where she is?"

"I do!" chimed half a dozen voices, and Noah instantly found himself being ushered toward the open back door of apartment 4D. It was a little like crowd surfing with a band of dwarves.

"Miss Ava, Miss Ava! Look who's here!" the children called as they all but shoved him across the threshold. The smell of cooking food assaulted his senses—too many scents to name—and his mouth began to water.

"Did you find him?" a woman called from the small kitchen, and Noah heard the oven door close with an unholy screech.

He really should find a way to fix that.

Ava Campbell stuck her head around the corner, and her whole face lit up at the sight of her only son and his entourage. "Good work, kids!" she said as she wiped her hands on a dish towel. Noah's young companions scattered, their job done, and he was able to wrap his arms around his mother for the first time since the semester began. His near-constant work schedule and unreliable car didn't encourage many trips home.

"So, your fan club remains," his mom observed, and Noah gave a self-deprecating shrug.

"Yeah, but don't tell anyone at school; you'll ruin my image."

His mother snorted and pulled out of his embrace far enough to begin her inspection. "You look tired, honey," she said, running her hands along his shoulders the way mothers often did. "Are you getting enough sleep? And is your hair . . . blue?"

Noah waved her concern away with a careless hand. "Sleep is for the weak," he insisted. "And sort of." He left a quick kiss on the top of her head before stepping toward the kitchen, where he found the counters laden with produce and supplies. Three pots bubbled quietly on the stove, and the oven light revealed two casserole dishes visible through the small window.

"You know everyone is bringing food, right? Not just you?" he teased.

"Yeah, yeah, but you know how I am. Hungry bellies call, and I have to answer."

Noah lifted the lid of one pot and peeked inside without comment. Yes, he did know how his mother was. Cooking was her love language. She'd probably been a chef in another life—and almost in this one, too—but fate had had other plans.

He tried not to think about that.

"What can I do?" he asked, replacing the lid.

His mother smiled broadly and pointed to a wide silver chef's knife on the closest cutting board. "You can chop onions," she said, and Noah stifled a groan. He always had to chop the onions.

"You just like to see me cry," he grumbled good-naturedly. He moved to the sink and began to scrub his hands.

His mom only cackled. "It's good for you," she said. "A man who never sheds tears forgets how to comfort others."

"Confucius says . . ." Noah quipped.

She bumped him with her hip as she moved to the stove. "Hush!"

"I'm sorry! You sound like a fortune cookie," he protested. He shut off the faucet with his elbow the way his mother had taught him and reached for a roll of paper towels. Then he moved to the cutting board and picked up an already-peeled onion before chopping it neatly in half in one swift motion.

"That doesn't mean it isn't true," his mother answered.

The sound of pounding feet grew louder and then faded as one of the children ran past the open back door.

"Annie! Slow down!" a woman yelled, and Noah couldn't help but smile. Annie Hernandez had been in a hurry for every one of her seven years on this Earth. Noah remembered the night she was born; he'd been fifteen, and Mrs. Hernandez's screams of panic had woken him from a dead sleep.

That was also the night their gloomy apartment complex had started to become a tribe.

His mother had rushed across the patio in her pajamas to bang on the frightened woman's door. Mrs. Kiernan in 5A had called an ambulance, and her husband had waited in the parking lot to flag it down. Mr. Huxley next door had made Julian, who was about to be a big brother, a steaming cup of hot chocolate to calm his nerves.

Annie had waited for the ambulance before making her appearance, but only just. Noah had been on the patio when she'd started to cry.

From that day forward, people had begun to speak when they'd passed each other outside, as if the events of that night had forged some unseen bridge between strangers. Neighbors who had been neighbors for years finally learned each other's names.

And Noah's mom had started to cook.

First, of course, she'd taken care of the Hernandezes, slowly filling their fridge and freezer to prepare for the exhausting months ahead while they tended to their newborn. Then, she'd started cooking for the others. Cookies for the kids, casseroles for the working mothers, meat pies for the old men.

And, almost like magic, the favors began to return.

Mr. Romano, after enjoying a sausage quiche, offered to fix their leaky kitchen window. Mrs. Everleen, smitten with Noah's mother's raspberry tarts, patched the torn knees of Noah's school jeans. Nobody had much to spare, but little by little, one person's talent met another person's need—and they discovered that life was better together.

Now, doors were open as often as the weather would allow. Children from one unit could often be found in another, and meals and chores and carpools were shared whenever possible. It was a different world from the one Noah and his mother had moved into on that drizzly evening so many years before. And somehow, all it had taken was a baby.

Ironically, the same thing that had forced them there in the first place.

Noah scored half the onion in parallel lines, then curled the ends of his fingers so that the tips pressed against the vegetable's white flesh. The knife flashed as the flat part of the blade moved against his knuckles and made a satisfying click against the wooden board beneath it. His eyes began to burn and water, but he resisted the urge to wipe them with the back of his wrist.

"Good to know you can still chop like a pro," his mother commented from the far side of the stove.

Noah gave a half smile. "It's hard to forget years of you yelling 'don't chop your fingers off!' every fifteen seconds."

"Well, you still have all ten of them, so I must have done

something right," she went on. "Besides, women like men who can cook, so I did you a favor."

Noah grunted as an image of Olivia flashed across his mind. He wondered if he'd ever have a reason to cook for her.

"When you get done with that, go ahead and take the dishes from the oven and put them on the big table outside. I've got to make room for the stuffing," his mother went on.

Noah scraped his diced onion into a smaller bowl and obediently donned a pair of thick oven mitts. One by one, the dishes, all cooked to perfection, made their way to the community table, where they waited for dinnertime under aluminum-foil tents. When all was ready, everyone sat down in long lines on either side of the feast while a dozen conversations tangled together. Then, a tinkling sound began at the far end of the table.

"Hear ye, hear ye!" Mr. Huxley called. "I proclaim it time for the annual giving of thanks. I'll go first. I'm thankful to still have two good legs to stand on, though one is admittedly better looking than the other."

Everyone around the table laughed, since it was well known that Mr. Huxley had a prosthetic leg.

"Now, go this way," he ordered, gesturing to his right.

Mrs. Kiernan pushed back her chair and stood up. "I'm thankful to have two new grandbabies this year, both healthy."

The tradition continued down the line, and other neighbors mentioned their health, their friends and, of course, the ability to feed their families for another season. Finally, it was Noah's turn. He casually pushed his chair back and rose to stand.

"This year, I am thankful for mail," he said.

There was a confused sort of pause around the table.

"For mail?" Mr. Kiernan asked, and Noah nodded. He cleared his throat, the anticipation making his mouth dry.

"Yes, for mail. Specifically, for the letter saying I've been accepted to grad school at UT Chattanoo—"

He didn't get to finish, because his mother leapt from her chair like it was on fire.

"NOAH JAMES!" she shouted. He staggered as she threw her arms around him with more force than he was expecting. "You're gonna be a doctor!"

"Of physical therapy," he clarified. "But yes."

The table burst into applause and excited chatter, only some of which he could hear over his mother's babbling.

"How long have you known? When do you start? Why didn't you tell me!?" she asked.

"Next fall," he said, returning her hug. "And I wanted to surprise you."

She grumbled something about his timing, though her cheeks were wet and her smile was happy when she pulled away. "I am so proud of you! I knew you would do it."

Noah felt a hot prickling sensation along the bridge of his nose, which only got worse when he looked around the patio. Mrs. Hernandez was dabbing her eyes with a napkin, and Mr. Huxley was nodding his head, as if he'd known this day would come all along. Noah's family, such as it was, was beaming at him.

These were the people who meant the most to him in the world—the ones who had been there through the hardest times of his life.

So why could he only think about the one who wasn't there?

He accepted all the congratulations and praise his neighbors heaped upon him, wearing them like a cape for the rest of the meal. He put on a big smile and twirled the little ones high in the air like helicopters. He made his usual jokes. But somehow, it all felt hollow.

And he knew his mother could tell.

When they were finally alone in their quiet kitchen, his mom deftly washing the many dishes and Noah drying beside her, he kept his eyes on the speckled countertop and waited.

At last, she cleared her throat. "Honey, let it out," she said simply.

Those four words gave Noah permission to open the box where he stuffed all the things he didn't want to think about—the things that rarely saw the light of day.

"I want to tell him," he said. The words felt sharp in his throat, like pieces of glass, and he clamped down on the sudden wave of emotion that surged into his chest. "I hate him so much I can't breathe, but I still want to tell him. And I wish I didn't."

Noah heard the clink of dishes touching the bottom of the sink, and then the faucet turned off. His mother's warm fingers, still damp from the water, moved against the side of his face, turning it—and the rest of his body—toward her. He stepped into her hug like he was a little boy again and not a grown man of almost twenty-three.

"Honey, don't let him take this from you," she said softly. Her hands moved along his spine in a comforting rhythm. "You deserve to get what you want."

"Do I?" Noah asked, his cheek resting against her temple.

"Yes," she said firmly, "you do. Noah, your father made the biggest mistake of his life when he chose not to be part of yours. You are a good man."

"But I'm just like him!" Noah blurted, unable to help himself. "Everybody always said so."

"You are the *good* things about your dad. You're his persistence, his dedication. You're his brains, his sense of humor . . . his loyalty."

Noah scoffed. "Like that means anything," he muttered.

"Honey," his mother started, pulling out of his arms. She looked up at him with the same blue-gray eyes he saw in the mirror every day. "The Ian Campbell *I* knew loved you fiercely. From the day you came into this world—screaming to wake the dead—he was so proud of you. He knew you would do great things with your life, and maybe . . ."

She paused, like she wasn't sure how to go on. "Maybe that's why he left. Maybe he knew you and I were strong enough to be okay."

Noah couldn't believe his ears. He stared down at his mother with his mouth hanging open. "*What?*" he breathed.

"I'm not saying it's okay! What he did to us was unforgivable," she went on quickly. "But, I don't know, maybe I've made peace with it. Well, not peace, exactly, but I've come to terms with the fact that it wasn't my fault. It wasn't *your* fault. We didn't do anything to deserve—"

"No, we didn't!" Noah said, hearing his volume rising. "We didn't deserve to have our lives turned upside down! To lose our house! To work ourselves to the bone scrubbing toilets and flipping burgers and walking every flea-ridden dog in five miles just to patch the tires on a car that's falling apart at the seams!"

"Noah . . ."

"You were supposed to have a restaurant!" he went on, the floodgates opened. "You were supposed to earn Michelin Stars! I was supposed to play baseball! I should be able to come see you more than four times a year! And now . . . now that I'm doing something with my life, I can't even enjoy it because all I want to do is find him and rub it in his face!" Noah stopped, panting as if he'd run a mile.

The silence following his outburst was heavy, and Noah fixed his gaze on the opposite wall and waited for the dust to settle.

When he could finally look down again, he saw quiet tears track down his mother's cheeks, and a wave of shame hit him in the chest. He was supposed to be the happy one, the comic relief. It wasn't his job to remind her how hard their lives had become; she could look around and see that for herself.

"Baby, you can't live like this," she said at last, wiping her cheeks with the heels of her hands. "You have to be able to go after what you want without letting the past weigh you down. We're in a good place now."

Noah rolled his eyes toward the ceiling, his jaw set tight.

"We *are*," his mother insisted. "Maybe it's not the same place we would have been in if he hadn't made the choice he did. Maybe there's an alternate universe out there somewhere where everything is different, but that doesn't mean we aren't okay right now. I have a steady income, and I'm getting to cook, even if it's not with my name on the front doors. You have a reliable job and an almost-finished college degree, and you've been accepted to graduate school in a field you love. You didn't play college ball on a full scholarship, but you plowed your way through the barriers with a determination that inspires me. *You* did that! You, not him. What you've earned is your own; don't let him take it from you. He does not deserve it."

Noah set his jaw and tried not to remember the night he'd stood on the curb after baseball practice and waited for his dad to pick him up, not yet knowing how everything was about to change. Those had been the last normal minutes of his life; the last ones where he felt whole and undamaged. Maybe one day he'd forget the wave of betrayal that had washed over him when he'd finally walked home and found his father's keys and cell phone on the counter beside a list of feeble excuses. Maybe he'd be able to wash his mind clean and learn how to forgive.

Maybe one day.

But not yet.

7

NOAH CAME HOME from work the Monday after Thanksgiving and crept through his own house like a burglar. Jake's truck was in the driveway, and the last thing Noah wanted to do was make enough noise to bring him downstairs. Something had clearly happened with Lexie over the holiday, though all Noah really knew was that his best friend had become a ticking time bomb, and life was easier when he made himself scarce.

He quietly assembled a sandwich and took his plate and a soda to the safety of his bedroom before pulling out his phone.

NOAH: How's Lexie?

OLIVIA: Still crying. How's Jake?

NOAH: Not good. He threw a box of loose sockets at the garage wall yesterday.

OLIVIA: Poor guy.

NOAH: What actually happened?

OLIVIA: I don't know. She went to his house for Thanksgiving, met his family, was having a blast and then . . . this.

NOAH: Well, Jake didn't do anything.

OLIVIA: How can you be so sure?

NOAH: Because he's totally whipped. I couldn't pay him to spill her milkshake.

OLIVIA: Don't say he's whipped. That's so condescending.

NOAH: Alright, fine. He's lost his mind over a girl, and he's going to further destroy my house because of it.

NOAH: Better?

OLIVIA: Much.

NOAH: I guess this makes me the enemy, huh?

OLIVIA: Yeah. It does.

NOAH: Well, that could be fun. ;)

OLIVIA: I wish you could see how hard I'm rolling my eyes right now.

NOAH: I can be there in ten minutes.

OLIVIA: Go to bed, Campbell. I'm not allowed to have wild animals in the house.

NOAH: Aw! But I'll sleep at the end of your bed, and I'm totally housebroken.

OLIVIA: Well, that's something at least.

NOAH MADE HIS way quietly along the next-to-last row of bookshelves on the library's second floor, an odd buzz of anticipation coursing through his veins. He'd finished his last final exam that morning. He had the night off work. There was absolutely *no* rational reason for him to be on campus again until the end of January . . . but he couldn't help it. He felt like an addict who needed another hit—just *one more night* to get him through the holiday break.

He paused at the end of the ancient history section when Olivia's table came into view. There she was, just as he'd expected—her books spread out on the wooden surface and her hair secured almost haphazardly with a bright-red clip along the back of her head. Several tendrils had already escaped, and they hung like wisps around her face as she leaned forward, her chin resting on the heel of one hand. There was something about that look—the one that was both careless and intentional—that drove Noah crazy. Maybe it was the idea that such a put-together woman could come undone.

Olivia reached for a neon-green highlighter and moved the tip across a sentence in her book. "I know you're standing there," she said, without looking up.

Noah shook his head and made his way toward the empty seat across from her. "Were you waiting for me, Pix?" he asked as he sat down. He reached his hand hesitantly toward her open bag of popcorn, which he noticed was now out in the middle of the table. It had started the week securely in her lap, so in some small way it felt like he was making progress.

"I've made peace with the inevitable," she mumbled. She glanced up, and her gaze caught on his hand as it inched toward her snack, but she made no move to stop him.

Noah grinned and tossed a handful of still-warm kernels into his mouth. "You know, if you really wanted to get rid of me, you would sit somewhere else."

"Too much work," she acknowledged with a sigh.

"Or maybe you don't actually want to get rid of me that badly," he suggested.

Olivia made a noncommittal sort of noise that wasn't an agreement or an objection.

Noah decided to take it as a win. He watched as she returned to her book, and her lips moved ever so slightly, like she was reading to herself. She frowned again and circled something with her highlighter. He wasn't cruel enough to distract her while she was legitimately focused, so instead he contented himself with eating her food and watching people stroll through the quad out the large window behind her.

It was creepy to stare at a person while they worked, after all.

But, despite his best efforts, his attention kept drifting back to her, like a magnet intent on finding true north. Her fruity perfume burrowed into his brain and wrapped around the memory that had lived there rent free for nearly three weeks: the quiet hush of that thrift store; the way the pulse in her wrist had pounded; the blaze of fire in her eyes when he'd leaned in.

"Don't kiss me," she'd said. How was it that three simple words—and negative words, at that—could play on repeat through so many different daydreams? He still wasn't sure how he'd managed not to pin her against a wall and kiss her until she couldn't walk a straight line. He'd only meant to get under her skin—maybe give her a reason to think about him after the afternoon was over.

Talk about backfiring.

Olivia finally sat up straight and shook her arms out by her sides. "I need a break," she muttered.

"I give massages," he offered, but Olivia met his hopeful expression with a skeptical one of her own.

"No thanks."

Noah pushed his lip out in a childish pout. "But what's the point of having me here if I can't help you with anything?"

"I'm still trying to figure that out," she shot back, and he couldn't help but grin.

He reached forward and took a single kernel of popcorn from the package of Orville Redenbacher's best. He'd slowed down his own consumption to be sure she'd have enough left for the rest of her evening, but no sooner had his hand touched the bag than she leaned over and pulled a gallon-sized Ziploc of kettle corn from her backpack. He stared in both amusement and surprise as she unzipped the top and started munching as if this were completely normal behavior. "Has anyone ever told you that you have a problem?" he asked.

She shrugged. "Corn is a vegetable."

"Yeah, *corn* is a vegetable, but the salt and butter it's covered in are not."

She held a piece of her emergency stash up to the light before tossing it into her mouth. "This is made with brown sugar," she pointed out.

Noah simply shook his head. There was no reasoning with this woman when it came to popcorn.

"Is this your last exam?" he asked instead, nodding toward the open book on the table. The upside-down chapter headers suggested a topic on abnormal child psychology.

Olivia let out a tired-sounding sigh. "Yeah. One more tomorrow, and then the girls and I are spending a week in the mountains."

Noah leaned forward earnestly. "You're sure you can't fit me in your suitcase?" he joked.

Her expression did not change. "Yes, I'm sure. This is a girls-only trip; no boys allowed."

"But I'm not a boy, I'm a man."

"Not until you're thirty, remember? And besides, they'll have men there."

Noah grunted and leaned back, stretching his legs out beneath the table. One of his boots bumped against hers, and he brought his ankles together—trapping her feet between his calves.

She met his challenging gaze and narrowed her eyes. Then she shifted in her seat, and the boots she'd been wearing went limp. He glanced beneath the table and found them empty, while both her socked feet were tucked underneath her, cross-legged.

Noah felt his face fall. "You're no fun," he grumbled, and Olivia shook her head slowly, as if humoring a small child.

"What is it you think you want from me, Campbell?" she asked. "I don't have time for a relationship."

"Well, then don't worry," he replied flippantly. "I'm not picturing you in any long white dresses. Short *black* dresses, however . . ."

Olivia popped another handful of kettle corn into her mouth. "Okay, then are you fishing for a friends-with-benefits situation? Because that's not going to happen, either."

He smirked. "I want to know if you ever think about the *almost*," he said, and a flicker of something foreign crossed her face—something very close to guilt.

Like maybe that was *exactly* what she'd been thinking about.

"No," she said, though she glanced down at her textbook as she did. "You and I are *just friends*, Campbell, and that's how it's going to stay."

Noah did his best to rein in a smile. "Say that again, Pix, with more conviction this time," he taunted.

Olivia looked up, embers flaring to life in her eyes. "I *said* we are just friends, and that's how it's going to stay. Whatever headway you think you've made with me is futile."

He rose to his feet and rounded the end of the table, keeping his eyes on hers as if stalking his prey. She sat with her arms crossed over her chest, every bit of her body language warning him to keep his distance, but pushing her buttons had become his new favorite pastime, and he loved the sparks that ignited when he found the right ones.

He pushed his luck to the point of recklessness and stepped behind her chair, her sharp, sweet perfume pulling him in like a bee to a flower—exactly as it had in the store. He tweaked one of those tempting tendrils along her jaw and then leaned down until his mouth was right beside her ear. "I think about the *almost*, Pix. All the time," he admitted softly.

She whipped her head around then, her mouth open to say something in reply, but Noah didn't wait to hear what it was. Instead, he flashed her a smile and turned his back, making his way down the aisle in the direction he'd originally come. "Try not to miss me!" he called over his shoulder.

An unmistakable huff of female anger punctuated his challenge, and he chuckled as he turned toward the lobby stairs. He didn't have Olivia Cohen all figured out—far from it, in fact—but he *did* know she was a bad liar.

And she had *definitely* thought about it.

❧

OLIVIA CHECKED HER phone the next afternoon as her plane pulled into the gate at the small airport in Jackson Hole, Wyoming. There were two messages from her parents; one from her brother, Danny; and another from Noah. Apparently, he'd rigged the creepy doll to drop from the ceiling of Conner's closet, and its appearance had prompted the invention of a few new words.

Noah's voice filled Olivia's mind as she read the other texts. *"I think about the almost, Pix. All the time."*

She shook her head and tried to banish the memory as she

pulled her backpack from under the seat in front of her. Noah Campbell was getting too close for comfort. It wasn't like he was the first guy to ever catch her attention, but he *was* the first one to really get under her skin like this, and it needed to stop. Winter break was the perfect chance to conduct a personal detox—a two-month Noah Campbell cleanse.

The simple truth was that, even if she were in the market for a man, she and Noah wanted very different things. She wanted someone serious, and he wanted a girl who would entertain him. He'd find somebody willing to play that part soon enough; all she had to do was keep him at arm's length until he did.

It was simple: out of sight, out of mind. Problem solved.

"Hey, Liv, can you grab my bag?" her friend Robin asked from across the aisle. She pointed to an overhead bin just ahead of where Olivia and Lexie were sitting.

"Yeah, sure thing," Olivia replied, rising to her feet. She slid her phone back into the pocket of her jacket before reaching to retrieve first Robin's bag and then her own. The small plane was filled with the normal hustle and bustle of people all anxious to get out of the cramped space and off to whatever adventures awaited them, and Olivia made a decision right then and there: she was not going to spend this girls' trip worrying about Noah-anything.

He simply wasn't worth the aggravation.

THURSDAY, DECEMBER 15

NOAH: I guess you guys are home because Lexie is here.

NOAH: Jake answered the door. No screaming. I think the Cold War might be over.

NOAH: Which is good because now we can go on that second date.

OLIVIA: Your wishful thinking is adorable.

NOAH: I'm told it's part of my appeal.

OLIVIA: You have a peel? That sounds like a personal problem.

NOAH: Ha ha. You're not funny.

✒

SATURDAY, DECEMBER 24

NOAH: See you tomorrow, Pix.

OLIVIA: ??

NOAH: You're what I asked Santa for. I've been a good boy this year.

OLIVIA: Keep dreaming, Campbell.

NOAH: Oh, trust me, I will.

8

"INCOMING," RILEY WARNED, her voice low as she turned her back and started randomly straightening the magazines in front of her register—anything to look busy. Noah stiffened, his hands automatically clenching around the edge of the checkout stand as he fought the urge to turn around. Meeting this problem head-on wouldn't make any difference.

"Campbell!" Simon bellowed from somewhere behind him. "If you let one more cart go out that door without your hands on it, I will personally hang you from the rafters in the deep freezer!"

Heat rose in Noah's neck, and he took a long, slow breath before turning to face his manager. He'd lost track of the number of times he'd been yelled at that afternoon; it was almost like Simon had a reprimand quota and only four hours left to meet it. "I've offered to help every customer, sir," Noah answered, nearly choking on the last word. "Sometimes they say no."

Simon gaped, peering up at Noah through close-set eyes that made him look a little like a ferret—a very ugly, very sweaty ferret. "I don't care what they say!" he screeched. "You walk them out anyway!"

A vision of Olivia flashed across Noah's mind, and her voice taunted him from months before. "But isn't running off with someone's groceries sort of like stealing?" he asked.

Simon planted his hands on his hips as a pair of obvious armpit stains inched their way across his white polo shirt. "It's the Watson's way," he hissed, "and you'd do well to remember where you work before you don't work here anymore." He jammed his index finger into Noah's breastbone, punctuating each word as he spoke. "Every. Cart. Got that?"

Noah glanced down the bridge of his nose, eyeing the smaller man's finger where it still rested against his vest. "Yes, sir," he answered tightly, and Simon's eyes widened, as if he'd just realized the young man he was bullying had at least four inches on him.

"Good," he snapped, though his voice was slightly higher than before. He opened his mouth again, like he had something else to say, but apparently thought better of it. Instead, he turned and stalked toward his office before stepping inside and slamming the door behind him.

Noah closed his eyes and finally let out the breath that had been lodged in his chest. *It's not a you thing, it's a him thing*, he chanted to himself, remembering the mantra that had gotten him through high school. The demon had been different then, but the context felt the same.

"He shouldn't lay into you like that," Riley said, reminding him where he was standing. "That last customer only had a box of tampons and a bottle of Advil, it's not like she needed your help—or probably wanted it, for that matter."

Noah made a conscious effort to relax his jaw. "But it's the Watson's way," he parroted with disgust. He was already counting the days until he could toss his name tag in the trash and walk out those front doors without looking back.

But, until then, he was stuck.

"I need more snakes," he muttered darkly, and Riley gave him a stern look.

"You *need* to keep your head down," she corrected. "The snakes only aggravated his chihuahua complex."

Noah coughed out a surprised laugh. "His *what?*"

"His chihuahua complex. You know, when a short guy wants to be the big man on campus, so he snaps at everyone's ankles and barks until somebody kicks him? Like a chihuahua."

Noah felt a reluctant smile tug at the corners of his mouth. "I think you mean a *Napoleon* complex," he said.

Riley waved her hand dismissively. "Chihuahuas make more sense. Besides, that's exactly what he looks like with those beady little eyes."

Noah shook his head and wiped one hand down his face, then he glanced toward the still-closed door of Simon's office. "What are we going to do for the next two hours?" he asked.

"Well, I don't know about you, but I'm going to redo all the things I've done in the last thirty minutes and look like I am very, very busy until closing. It's not like anyone's shopping right now," Riley answered. Then she put a new bag in the trash can behind her cashier's stand, even though the old one wasn't full.

Noah looked around and confirmed there were no customers in sight. Simon would probably find a way to make that his fault, too, even though nobody in their right mind was still grocery shopping after 8 p.m. on New Year's Eve. He sighed. If he didn't find something to do with his hands, he'd either be sent home early or, in Simon's current mood, fired—and neither option was good for his bank account.

"I'll get the broom," he muttered, and then he headed toward the supply closet at the back of the store. He'd made it halfway down aisle four before someone called his name.

"Noah!"

He turned toward the sound and saw Misty, one of the young women who worked in the bakery, hurrying past the oatmeal display. He sighed inwardly and pasted on a smile. It wasn't that Misty was annoying; she was actually very sweet. But she'd also once brought him cookies with his initials in curly blue icing and then claimed to have been "practicing her piping skills."

"There you are," she said, slightly out of breath as she came closer. "I checked up front, but Riley said you'd come this way."

"What can I do for you?" he asked as nicely as he could.

"I wanted to see if you have plans tonight—you know, since it's New Year's?"

Noah held in a snort. All his friends were out of town with their families, and he wouldn't make it home to Hampton before the new year officially began. He'd probably ring it in alone in his own house eating microwaveable chicken wings like he did most years. Not that he really cared—January would come whether he welcomed it or not. "Nah, I'm gonna head home. It's been a long night," he answered. He took a few steps toward his destination, and Misty fell into rhythm beside him.

"Well, my roommates are actually throwing a party right now, so I'm heading back to a madhouse. There's usually a keg," she said. "You could stop by if you want. Unwind a little."

Noah pushed open the swinging door to the stockroom and held it for her, since she obviously intended to follow. The look on her face was so hopeful it made him pause. Why not go to Misty's party? Have a beer, make some new friends, maybe get to know her a little better? He could certainly do worse.

The door swung closed behind them, and she stepped into his personal space. "You might get more than a midnight kiss," she murmured, looking him dead in the eye as she did.

And there it was.

He remembered the cookies and all the not-so-subtle hints about movies she'd like to see and restaurants she enjoyed . . . It was just too easy. Where was the challenge? Where was the adrenaline rush?

He thought of Olivia and wondered what she was doing for the holiday. Now *there* was a girl who wouldn't be won easily. Not that Noah wanted to *win* her, but still. She kept him on his toes, made him work for every inch he gained—and the little victories felt like conquering the world.

Noah stepped around Misty where she was planted in his path and finally reached the supply closet and retrieved a wide push broom. "Thanks for the invite, but I can't. I'm sorry," he said.

The disappointment on her face was palpable. "Oh. But I thought you're just going home?" she asked.

Noah took a slow breath and tried to decide how to spin the truth without hurting her feelings too much. Yes, he was just going home, but turning down her offer was about more than that. "Misty, I'm just not sure it's a good idea. I mean, we do work together."

"There aren't rules about that," she countered.

Wow, she wasn't going to make it easy, was she?

"No, but still. Just trust me."

She chewed on one side of her lip and shifted her weight to the other foot. "But—"

Noah reached out and tweaked a piece of her hair that had fallen around her face—a motion that only made Olivia brighter in his mind. "Enjoy your party, Misty," he said, and he offered a smile before turning toward the door. He'd already been away from the registers far longer than he'd intended, and he didn't need to stick around to watch Misty process the rejection.

He hurried back toward the registers, pushing the broom ahead of him. Normally he would zigzag his way through the store from front to back, sweeping as he went, but that would probably mean running into Misty as she left, which he definitely wanted to avoid.

"Where have you been?" Riley hissed as he pushed the broom past her register. "I was about to send out a search party!"

"Have you had customers?" he asked.

"No, but Simon's been out here barking orders like a drill sergeant, and he knows you were missing. What happened?"

Noah saw motion at the edge of his vision and looked up to see Misty hurrying out the front doors, her head ducked down inside the collar of her jacket. He nodded discreetly in her direction, and Riley followed his gaze. "Misty cornered me in the stockroom and made me an offer I had to refuse."

Riley turned back and looked at him with wide eyes. "Are you serious?"

"Yeah."

"Poor thing." Riley lifted onto her tiptoes to peer through the front windows, as if she could still see the other girl's retreat. "She's really sweet on you, you know."

"Oh, really? I hadn't figured that out," Noah said dryly. "She invited me to a party at her place."

"And you have plans?"

"Well, no."

"But you're not interested?"

"Well . . . yes."

"Yes, you're not interested, or yes, you *are* interested?" Riley repeated, and Noah felt agitation rising in his chest.

"Would you stop?" he snapped. "I don't do the girlfriend thing, and Misty has 'girlfriend' written all over her. It's just a problem waiting to happen."

"Alright, alright," Riley said, her hands up in surrender. "I get it. No need to bark at me."

Noah pushed the broom past the end of her register and up the other side before returning to his starting position. "Sorry," he muttered. Then he sighed loudly. "Maybe I do need to blow off some steam."

"Yeah, maybe," she said. She scrubbed a wad of paper towels against a shiny spot where something had spilled on her conveyor belt. "You could come out with Bryce and me tonight," she added.

"And third-wheel it? No, thanks."

"No, we're going to a party," Riley explained. "I don't even know who's hosting; some girl from Bryce's nutrition class sent a blanket invitation to the whole department. Apparently, she's got a huge place somewhere on the other side of town and is pretty well-known for her events."

Noah grimaced at the thought of a stranger's loud, crowded house. "Eh, I don't know," he hedged.

"Well, you could also go home and marinate in the Simon-ness of this night," Riley said thoughtfully, as if she were really weighing the options. "But at least this way you're not drinking alone."

Noah and his broom did another circuit of the registers, weaving back and forth between each one while he considered the invitation. His mind wandered back to Olivia and the many questions he'd asked himself since she'd left town. Was there something specifically wrong with him that had turned her away? Was he not good enough somehow? Did she already have somebody else? He shook his head hard to banish the thoughts before they could take hold. If he went home alone, he'd have almost no choice but to consider the possibilities—an option that was even less desirable than Misty's offer. Finally, he made his choice.

"Alright," he told Riley as he passed by again. "But I'll drive myself."

"Deal," she said.

Noah turned and pushed the broom toward aisle one, ready to start his winding path through the store before closing. He already felt like he might regret his decision, but what was done was done.

And who knew? Maybe the night would surprise him.

THE STEADY THUMP of R&B music followed Olivia as she made her way across the back patio of an old, ivy-covered house. Floor-to-ceiling windows spilled light across the sloping lawn and gave a glimpse into the packed living area where fifty or sixty people were moving to the beat of the speakers. It was too loud, too crowded, too *much*, but Robin never could resist the need for extravagance.

Olivia wrapped the edges of her coat around herself and exhaled a breath that hovered white in the air for a moment before dissipating into the dark. The click of her heels seemed unusually loud as she hurried across the immaculate paving stones. She seemed to be the only person outside.

The only person stupid enough to be outside, you mean.

Olivia huffed at the condescending voice in her own mind. She'd given the party a solid hour, but her social battery was empty. Unfortunately, Robin's room was directly above the DJ stand, and there was no way Olivia would find any peace there—closed doors or not.

She swiftly glanced over her shoulder to make sure she hadn't been followed and then stepped off the edge of the patio and scampered around the corner of the house. Robin's mother had what Robin called "delicate nerves," and nowhere in her husband's massive house had proven relaxing enough for her disposition. As a result, Mrs. Kline had her own outdoor retreat—a small summer house at the edge of the property. It was shielded from view by a row of tall cedar trees, which still boasted evergreen needles at this time of year. Olivia followed a paved path through the branches and breathed a sigh of relief when she came out the other side and saw that the little house was dark.

Apparently, none of the other partygoers had found the hideaway yet. Hopefully, it would stay that way.

She checked behind her again, feeling a little like a thief as she stole toward the secret haven. There was nothing she wanted more in that moment than peace and quiet—and to take her shoes off. Olivia climbed two small steps to the door and raised the latch, which Robin had told her would be unlocked. She slid the door open and slipped in through the gap before shutting it quietly behind herself. She really didn't *need* to be quiet, seeing as how she was the only one there, yet she couldn't bring herself to break the stillness that hovered in the air.

She turned at last and pressed her back against the door, finally feeling the thump of the bass speakers fade into the recesses of her mind. It was only then that she realized the dark room was already warm, when it should have been cold.

"Don't freak out," someone said quickly. "It's only me."

Olivia's hands flew to her mouth, stifling an instinctive shriek as a lamp clicked on.

"I'm sorry, Pix. There wasn't any good way not to scare you," the unwelcome figure said from his spot on the couch.

Olivia surveyed Noah with wide eyes, and the pieces of her brain that hadn't gone into flight mode scrambled to understand his sudden appearance. "How did you—? Where did—? What—?" she stammered as too many questions tried to come out all at once. She took a deep breath and tried to slow the hammering of her heart. *Why did he keep doing that!?*

"Why are you sitting in the dark?" was the question that finally fought its way to the surface—though, on second thought, it probably wasn't the most pressing.

Noah gave a pained sort of smile and pushed one hand back through his hair, which was already standing on end. "I'm hiding," he admitted.

Olivia glanced out one of the wide windows, almost expecting to see a wild animal she'd somehow missed before. "From what?" she asked.

Noah gestured toward the house in the direction she had come. "Probably from the same thing you're hiding from."

She took a step into the room and finally took in her surroundings. Noah was sitting on one of two comfortable-looking sofas that faced each other over a glass coffee table. The lamp he'd turned on illuminated a carved wooden side table and matching desk in the far corner, which was bracketed by tall bookcases full of books with titles in gold foil. He'd obviously figured out how to turn on the heat, and the small space was cozy despite the winter chill outside. "So, you're a party guest?" she asked.

"Well, I'm not trespassing, if that's what you mean."

She shook her head, still coming to terms with the fact that he was even there to begin with. "No, I just didn't see you inside. And I didn't know you knew Robin."

"Who?"

"Robin Kline? The girl who lives here?"

"Oh. Well, I don't, actually. I came with friends from work, who I guess know her—or know *of* her, at least."

Olivia bit the inside of her cheek to hold in a snarky comment; Robin's mass invitations really got out of hand sometimes. She shrugged off the long peacoat she'd gotten for Christmas and reached to hang it on a rack near the door.

"Wow."

The single word slipped from Noah's lips as if by accident, and Olivia glanced down at her outfit like she was seeing it for the first time. Her top was red with long, split sleeves that fell from her elbows like lacy wings, and the fabric shimmered like a million little stars in the right kind of light. She'd paired it with black pants that hugged her curves and strappy heels that showed off a fresh pedicure. She looked good, and she knew it, but the shell-shocked expression on Noah's face made an unexpected surge of pleasure course through her veins.

Not that she actually cared what he thought, specifically, but it was nice to feel appreciated all the same.

"Close your mouth, Campbell. You're gonna catch flies," she warned.

His mouth, which had been slightly open, snapped shut, and she could see his throat work as he swallowed. "Sorry," he muttered, still watching intently as she crossed the colorful rug and sat on the couch opposite his. "I've just never seen you quite like that. I feel like I needed a heads-up."

"Too much for you, huh?"

What? Don't encourage him! she chided herself. Then she cleared her throat and crossed her legs. She'd intended to take off her shoes, but somehow that felt presumptuous now that she wasn't alone. "I didn't even know you were in town," she said. "I figured you'd gone home like everyone else who isn't local."

Noah huffed and swung his socked feet to the floor so he was facing her with his forearms on his knees. "Home is where the paycheck is, and vacations are when I make the big bucks," he explained.

"Oh, really?"

"Well, everyone else is gone, and somebody has to pick up the slack," he pointed out. "Might as well be me."

"Have you not seen your family at all?" she asked. The very idea of spending an entire holiday break alone in a college town was depressing to consider.

"The store was closed for two days at Christmas, so I saw my mom then," he explained. He must have seen the stricken look on her face, because he went on. "It doesn't bother me, actually. I have the whole house to myself, which means the dishes actually get washed and nobody eats my food. Conner's gone, so no booby traps, and I never have to wait in the drive-thru."

"Still, though. I'm sorry you don't get more of a break."

Noah shrugged as if it didn't matter. Then he gestured toward his black pants and white button-up shirt. "I just came from work, actually. That's why I look like a waiter."

That pulled a laugh from Olivia's throat. "Well, you could have kept your green vest on for color."

"Oh, yeah, and have people ask me if beer is on sale all night? That's a good idea," he quipped, and Olivia felt her smile stretch wider.

"So, I take it you didn't drive yourself here, since you're hiding instead of bailing?" she asked.

Noah scrubbed his palm across his face in obvious frustration. "No, I didn't. I was going to, but then my car wouldn't start so I caught a ride with Riley. I'm pretty much stuck here until she and Bryce decide to go home."

"Ah, that sucks," Olivia commiserated.

"What about you?"

"What?"

"Why are you hiding instead of bailing?" he asked.

"Oh, I'm actually staying the night. Robin is a friend of mine."

Noah nodded in silent understanding. "So, that's how you knew this place was out here."

"Yeah, I've been here before. How did you find it?"

"I was wandering—because that's what sad, lost little grocery boys do, right?"

His tone was biting, almost like he was berating himself for matching his own description, and Olivia felt her brow pinch in the middle as she considered him. He did look a little sad, and maybe somewhat lost, but mostly just very, very tired. There was silence as Noah stared down at the rug between his feet.

"You okay?" she finally asked.

Noah's shoulders rose as he drew in a breath, but he didn't answer.

"It's okay to *not* be okay, you know," she went on. Then she waved her hand to encompass the walls around them. "No shame here. Cone of silence. Expires at midnight."

His eyes drifted closed, and he pinched the bridge of his nose between two fingers. Then he chuckled dryly. "You want to hear something funny?" he asked.

Olivia blinked in surprise. That was not the answer she'd expected to hear. "Uh, sure?" she replied.

"This morning, I was attacked by somebody's grandmother."

She barked out a laugh and then clapped a hand over her mouth. "I'm sorry, you were *what*?"

He sighed and propped his elbows on his knees and his chin in his cupped hands. He sounded drained, but there was still a trace of his usual good humor on his face. "Alright, you want the long version or the short version?"

Olivia leaned back against the cushions and crossed her arms over her chest. "You got anyplace better to be?"

"No."

"Then the long version, for sure," she insisted.

A faint smile pulled at Noah's mouth. "Alright, well, like all ridiculous Watson's stories, this one starts with Simon."

"Of course."

"He told the new grocery supervisor black-eyed peas aren't that popular around here, and that we didn't need to worry about stocking any extra for the holiday."

"Are you serious?" Olivia interrupted. "New Year's Day is the only time black-eyed peas *are* popular!"

"I know, right? He's a genius," Noah went on. "Anyway, we ran out early in the week, and apparently, we can't restock now because every warehouse in the southeast is empty. So we had to enforce a limit: one bag or two cans of peas per paying customer, no exceptions."

Olivia snorted in disbelief. She, like every other good Southerner, would have ham and peas and collard greens in the morning to bring good luck for the new year. It was tradition, and had *been* tradition, for generations; any store having a purchase limit was bound to bring trouble.

"So, fast-forward to this morning," Noah continued. "I'm standing by my register when I hear yelling from aisle nine, which happens to be—"

"—where the peas are," Olivia finished.

"Exactly. So, Josh and I go over to investigate."

"Wait, who's Josh?"

"A guy from the stockroom," Noah clarified. "Anyway, we go over to see what the problem is, and this little old lady has four bags of peas in her cart—the last four bags from the shelf. Another older woman is yelling at her, pointing to all the limit signs and lecturing her on being selfish during a holiday. I try to politely point out that the second lady is right and we can only allow one bag per customer, but then the first woman shoves her cart at the second woman, who falls down. Then, she swings her purse at me and hits me square in the chest!"

"Poor baby!" Olivia cooed, but Noah went on as if she hadn't interrupted.

"Now, normally, this wouldn't be a problem since I'm built like a tank—"

"Naturally."

"—but this time, her bag was *heavy*! Like bricks-in-the-bottom heavy. And when it hit the floor, it *clanked*."

Olivia gave an exaggerated gasp.

"I know, right? So now we've got store security coming to break up an old lady fight *and* find out why her bag is making metallic noises. Turns out, she had three more cans of peas and a tub of frozen whipped cream in there! I have a bruise!"

Olivia couldn't help it—she laughed out loud. "You really were attacked by somebody's grandma!" she managed, forcing the words out between giggles.

"You thought I was lying, didn't you?" he accused, though he looked like he was trying not to smile. "I had to fill out an employee incident report and everything!" His face suddenly sobered. "And of course Simon felt the need to yell at me in front of the staff because apparently customer violence is somehow my fault."

Olivia pressed her lips together, her laughter all played out. "I'm sorry," she said.

"And then it was *also* my fault when some idiot almost backed his car into me in the parking lot because apparently it's hard to see a line of twenty shopping carts moving through your rear-view mirror," Noah bit out, looking back down at the floor. He sounded disgusted.

Olivia chewed on the inside of her cheek and thought about his story. "Maybe he deserved the snake," she admitted, and Noah's eyes flicked up to hers.

"Yeah, he did," he said with a sigh. "But he hated me before that." Then he leaned back, mirroring her position from across the coffee table. "And I should just be grateful to have a job, right? Even if the guy in charge uses me as a doormat?"

She tilted her head from one side to the other. "You're allowed to be upset about it," she acknowledged. "But graduation is coming, and then you'll be done, right?"

He sighed again and ran his hand down his face in resignation. "Yeah, but it can't come soon enough," he muttered.

Olivia circled one of her ankles and flexed her toes inside her heels. She'd never seen this side of Noah before—the one that wasn't all fun and games. It was actually a bit disconcerting. "If you could fast-forward time, would you?" she asked suddenly. It was one of the questions she and her brothers had debated many times on long car rides, and it felt relevant.

Noah looked at her for a moment, understandably confused. "What?"

She shrugged and flexed her ankles again. "It's pretty self-explanatory," she said. "If you had the power to fast-forward time and skip the parts you didn't like, would you do it?"

The expression on Noah's face shifted, and he actually seemed to be considering the question. "If I fast-forward, do I come out the other side knowing all the things I would have learned in the time I skipped or do I come out exactly as I am now, just older?" he asked.

This was a point she'd discussed before, and she was ready with her answer. "You come out as if that part of your life has happened, but you didn't actually experience it. So, if you fast-forward to graduation, you would have the knowledge without the hassle of actually going to class."

He furrowed his brow. "So . . . let's say I convinced you to go out with me during the time I skipped, I would wake up with a memory of a date, even though I didn't actually go on it?"

Olivia rolled her eyes. "For the sake of argument, yes."

"Hard pass, then. I definitely want to be there," he answered instantly.

"But—also for the sake of argument—what if we go on a whole bunch of dates and you fall desperately in love with me and then I break your heart into five thousand tiny little pieces? Wouldn't you want to skip that?"

"You're assuming, first of all, that I would fall in love with you, which is doubtful, and you're also assuming you'd be able to give me up after all that, which is also doubtful."

She huffed, now wishing she hadn't asked the question in the first place. "Okay, fine, forget I asked," she said, looking down at her feet. She pointed her toes and stretched her ankles again.

After a moment, there was motion in her peripheral vision, and she looked up to find Noah circling the end of the coffee table. "What are you doing?" she asked, instantly on alert.

He sat down at the far end of her couch, facing her with one knee pulled up onto the cushion. Then he reached a hand out, palm up, and curled his fingers inward. "Give 'em here," he insisted.

Olivia scanned his face, caught off guard by the sudden change of subject and dismayed to see that he was completely serious. "I'm sorry, what?"

"Your feet. I know they hurt; you've been stretching your arches since you sat down. So give 'em to me."

She let out a disbelieving laugh. "Uh, no, thank you," she replied, suddenly self-conscious. There was no way she was letting him touch her feet.

Noah pursed his lips before folding forward and reaching toward the floor. In one swift motion, he'd closed his hand around her left ankle and pulled it toward him, and Olivia yelped in surprise as her whole body swiveled ninety degrees. "I'm going to be a physical therapist; feet don't bother me," he explained matter-of-factly. Then he unfastened the dainty silver clasp on her ankle strap and slid the shoe off before dropping it to the floor with a thud.

Olivia only gaped, all protests dying on her lips as Noah took her bare foot in his warm hands, and she was immensely glad she'd decided to wear pants instead of a skirt. He pressed both thumbs near her heel and smoothed a slow path upward before curving out and starting over. Once, twice, three times. Every cell in her body was laser-focused on her foot, and she couldn't seem to take her eyes off his hands as they moved over her skin. When he crossed over a pain point, she hissed in a breath.

"Right there, huh?" His touch gentled instantly, and he moved in smooth circles over a knot in the muscle beneath his thumbs. "Try to relax, Pix. I'm not going to hurt you on purpose," he said.

"It's the accidental part I'm worried about," she mumbled, though her sarcasm switch seemed to be malfunctioning. It would have been easier to stop him if he'd been bad at this, but, unfortunately, he wasn't.

Another moment passed before she glanced up and caught him watching her face. His blue-gray eyes seemed to be looking for something. "Let me guess, I'm going to owe you after this," she said dryly.

He pressed his lips into a hard line, one that almost looked irritated. "No, Pix," he answered tightly. "You have a problem, and I can fix it. That's all. No sense in you being in pain all night." He released one foot and reached for the other without pause.

Olivia did her best not to melt into the sofa. She actually felt bad about her question; she'd meant to imply he had a motive, but she hadn't really meant to insult his character. The voices in her mind began debating how best to apologize, but she never got the chance.

"Would you rather eat food from a fancy restaurant or a gas station for the rest of your life?" he asked, breaking the now-tense silence, and she was grateful.

"Definitely a gas station," she said. "You can't get a burger and fries at a fancy restaurant."

He shrugged, his thumbs still working over the arch of her right foot. "Well, sometimes you can, but it'll probably have oysters or something on it."

"Exactly. Why mess with a good thing?"

"But if you eat from a gas station all your life, you will never leave the bathroom."

Olivia wrinkled her nose. The statement was unpleasant, even if it was true. "You have to be smart about it," she countered. "You obviously shouldn't eat sushi from a gas station, but burgers and tacos are usually alright."

"And you're going to eat burgers and tacos for the next sixty years?" he asked with raised eyebrows.

"I take it you'd choose the fancy restaurant?"

"Depends on the restaurant. Someplace that serves teeny, tiny portions that look like sea creatures? That's not going to work. But a good steakhouse with blooming onions and really good apps? I'd be down with that."

"So steak is your comfort food?" she asked.

He pressed the heel of his hand against the center of her foot. "Nah, my comfort food is Nutella toast with bananas," he admitted. "My mom used to make it when I was sick."

Olivia nodded, understanding the sentiment. "For me it's chicken and gravy with rice. Mom made it for dinner every time Dad got home from a mission, and it still makes me feel like everything will be okay."

Noah furrowed his brow. "Where would he go?"

"My dad? He was Special Forces for years, so he would just disappear—sometimes in the middle of the night—and we never knew exactly where he was or how long he'd be gone. Sometimes it was days, sometimes it was weeks, but he always came back."

A cloud seemed to pass behind Noah's eyes, though his expression remained neutral. "Sounds terrifying," he said.

"I didn't love it," she admitted, "but for us it was normal. An unsettling, bizarre sort of normal, I suppose. I never breathed easy until the chicken and gravy came out."

He gave her foot one final squeeze before setting it on the cushion beside him. Olivia briefly considered *not* taking up two-thirds of the couch but then dismissed the idea. She was comfortable, and he didn't seem to mind, so she tucked her bare feet under his leg and settled herself more fully against the throw pillows, feeling a little like the Queen of Sheba. It wasn't a terrible sensation.

"Would you rather live in a tree house and never come down or in an underground bunker and never come up?" she asked.

Noah chuckled softly, shaking his head, and Olivia felt his humor mirrored on her own face. "Alright, so if I lived in a tree house . . ."

Almost an hour passed before she even wondered what time it was.

"Wow, it's already eleven fifty-five!" she exclaimed after finally spotting a clock on one of the bookshelves.

Noah grunted in acknowledgement and stretched his arms toward the ceiling. "Well then, you've got five minutes to decide," he said.

"Decide what?"

"Whether or not you're going to kiss me at midnight."

She snorted. "Okay, done. I'm not going to kiss you at midnight," she said.

"Cone of silence, remember? Nothing that happens in here will follow us out there," he said, gesturing toward the closest window.

Olivia crossed her arms over her chest and leveled him with a serious stare. "We've talked about this, Campbell. I am not going out with you."

"And once again, Cohen, I'm not asking you out," he declared with a smirk. "But I do think you're going to kiss me anyway."

"And why is that?"

"Because I think you want to, whether you like it or not, and what better chance to try it out than on New Year's Eve when it doesn't have to mean anything?"

His voice was full of challenge, like he was daring her to protest, and Olivia found herself actually considering the possibility. He was right, one kiss didn't have to mean anything, especially if they agreed it wouldn't.

"But, I mean, if you don't think you can handle it, then that's a different story," he taunted.

"You talk a big game, Campbell, but what happens when you can't live up to your own hype?"

He shrugged. "It's never happened before."

The gleam in his eye grew brighter, and Olivia felt herself make an impulsive decision. She swung her bare feet to the floor and rose to stand. "Fine, I'll give you a chance to prove yourself," she said.

Noah shot to his feet beside her, and the sudden heat in his eyes made her ribcage tighten.

"But I have rules," she added.

He took a step forward, and she instinctively stepped back. She glanced at the clock. There were still three minutes until midnight, and she didn't have to let him into her bubble until then.

"Rules?" he asked, already looking a bit like a tiger on the prowl.

"Yes, rules," she repeated, taking another step back as he came closer. She held up her index finger as she counted. "One, your hands have to stay in neutral territory."

A sneaky smirk inched across his face, and one finger came up under her chin. He tipped her face up to his as he took another step forward. She moved again, but this time she felt the wall of the summer house against her back. A few choice words skittered through her mind; she hadn't meant to let him push her into a corner—figurative or otherwise.

Noah looked down at her like he was memorizing the details of her face, and his hand grazed back along her jaw toward the nape of her neck. While he was *technically* playing fair, it suddenly didn't feel like "neutral territory" at all.

"Okay," he murmured.

Olivia swallowed hard and reminded herself that this meant nothing. There was no reason he should affect her like this; none at all. "Two," she said, "this is *one* kiss. Once you break it, that's it. No repeats, no do-overs, no curtain calls."

He dipped his head, and Olivia felt the stubble on his chin graze the soft places on her neck. "Got it," he said, though it was really more of a breath that skated across her skin and sent a cascade of goose bumps down her spine.

She told herself to stay still, to give only what she'd agreed to and no more, but her subconscious didn't seem to be listening. Instead, she felt her head tilt to one side without her permission, as if some parts of her brain were staging a mutiny. She could feel her heart rate kick up another notch, and she tried to keep her mind from clouding over.

Why did he have to smell so good?

He skimmed slowly along her jaw and came to hover over her mouth, mere millimeters away as the clock ticked down. "Anything else?" he asked.

Olivia sort of thought she'd had a number three, but whatever it was vanished from her mind as both his hands threaded into her hair. She merely shook her head in response.

The final countdown started, and the chanting from the main house was so loud they could hear it where they stood.

Ten!

Nine!

"One chance. Don't choke," she reminded him, though it was hard to talk when she could barely breathe. She wasn't completely sure how she'd gotten into this predicament, but now that she was there, she could no more walk away than sprout wings and fly.

Eight!

Seven!

Noah pressed forward, pinning her completely against the wall, and Olivia felt her hands drift toward his waist of their own accord. The very air around them crackled with anticipation. "Stop talking," he commanded.

Six!

Five!

Four!

Olivia's eyes drifted closed.

Three!

Two!

One.

9

"**O**KAY, SO DON'T kill me because it wasn't my idea."

Olivia paused with her wooden spatula hovering over a large pan of vegetables. She cut her eyes toward where Lexie stood with her back against the edge of their kitchen counter. "*What* wasn't your idea?" she asked, her voice flat.

"Well, you know how I asked Jacob to come tonight?" Lexie began.

Olivia went back to cooking, the onions and garlic sizzling each time she stirred the skillet. She hadn't actually known her roommate's boyfriend was coming to their annual back-to-class dinner, but it wasn't surprising. Lexie and Jake's "Cold War," as Noah had called it, was definitely over, and the two of them could barely be separated on the best of days. "Sure," she replied.

"Well, Kate asked Jackson so there wouldn't be four girls and only one guy, since that's awkward," Lexie went on.

Olivia pursed her lips, suddenly getting a bad feeling about where this conversation was headed. "Sure . . ." she said again.

"Then, Robin wanted to ask that guy from her music class last semester, and . . . well, that would make an odd number, and she hates when things aren't balanced, so . . ."

Lexie was babbling now, and Olivia groaned. "So she picked somebody for me," she finished.

"Well . . . yes," Lexie admitted, and Olivia let out a deep sigh. Sometimes her friends couldn't leave well enough alone.

She dumped a package of frozen shrimp into the stir-fry and doused the whole thing in soy sauce. "Who is it this time?" she asked.

"Well, she wanted to ask some guy from her nutrition class—"

Olivia groaned again and squeezed her eyes shut. "I hate her nutrition friends," she complained. "They always want to mansplain carbs and proteins."

Lexie raised her shoulders. "That's what I said," she replied, "but she threatened to call him anyway if I didn't have a better idea."

Olivia muttered a few unkind words. "She could have asked *me*, you know," she said.

"Yeah, but it was just this morning, and you were in that orientation meeting at the Harrelson Center," Lexie went on. "Anyway, I suggested the first person I could think of who you wouldn't totally hate, and we asked and he happened to be free, so he's coming."

"Who did—"

Just then, the doorbell rang, and Lexie pushed away from the counter. "I'll get that," she said quickly, then she hurried from the room and left her roommate standing at the hot stove.

"Lexie! Who is—" Olivia shouted, but in the next moment, she heard the front door open, and a voice entered the apartment that made her question irrelevant. She'd really hoped to have more time before dealing with him again—like, the whole semester, if she was lucky.

But apparently, her luck hadn't lasted very long.

She straightened her spine and stirred the contents of the skillet with a vengeance as heavy footsteps came down the short hall. Someone stepped through the kitchen doorway and stopped. She didn't have to turn to know it was Noah; she could tell by the now-familiar scent of wintergreen and pine that had followed him into the room. The fact that she could associate a smell with him at all irritated her even more than his unexpected presence.

"Well, hey, Pixie!" he drawled. "See? I knew you'd ask for a second date sooner or later."

"I didn't ask you," she bit out. Then she glanced over her shoulder and surveyed him where he was leaning against the doorframe, his arms crossed over his chest as he watched her with a smirk that made the hair on the back of her neck stand on end. All at once, the memories she'd worked hard to keep at bay came flooding back: the press of his mouth over hers, the heat of his hands on her neck, the feel of his scruff against her face. A rush of warmth crept up her spine, and she went back to her cooking with a huff. "And this *isn't* a date," she added, just on principle.

Noah stepped farther into the room and came to stand behind her, as if looking over her shoulder while she worked. "Why are you mad at me, Pix? I haven't done anything yet."

"No, but you will," Olivia muttered darkly, "and then I'll have to put up with it."

"Put up with it?" he echoed, his voice far too smooth for her liking. "You didn't seem to just 'put up with it' the last time I saw you."

Olivia took a slow breath and tried to rein in the frustration she could feel building in her chest. It wasn't really about *him*; he could have been any guy from anywhere. It was about the way her body insisted on responding to him—the way she wanted to melt back against his chest like that was where she was supposed to be. It was infuriating, and she wouldn't have it! She flirted, sure, and she kissed, occasionally. But she didn't do . . . *this*.

Whatever *this* was, exactly.

"That's not going to happen again," she said firmly.

Noah moved imperceptibly forward, and she felt his chuckle against her shoulder blades. "What isn't?" he taunted, his voice full of false innocence. "Oh, you mean when I kissed you?"

Olivia pressed her lips together and swallowed, her attention fixed solidly on the stir-fry in front of her. "Yes."

"And when you kissed me back?"

She reached out and shut off the hot stove eye, probably using more force than necessary.

"Because you *really* kissed me back, Pix," he went on. "Like the world was ending and you only had five more seconds to—"

Olivia whirled around and sealed the palm of her hand over his mouth mid-word. The surprise on his face was gratifying. "What happened to 'nothing in here will follow us out there'?" she demanded. "It happened, okay? I'd rather not relive it."

His brow knit together down the middle, and she dropped her hand as she felt his smile fade. "Why not?" he asked, his humor now gone. "We didn't do anything wrong."

"Easy for you to say," she mumbled, not wanting to discuss the issue any further. She yanked open the silverware drawer, but Noah put his hand out and shoved it closed again.

"What does that mean?" he challenged. His gaze was piercing

as it raked over her face, like he was trying to decipher an answer from her expression.

Olivia searched for something she could say that would close the issue for good. She hated that she'd kissed Noah because it opened the door for drama, which was her least favorite thing in the whole world, and she simply didn't have the patience for it at this point in her life. But it also gave him a reason to think she would eventually . . .

She looked up into his eyes as a thought occurred to her—a devious, underhanded thought—but it took root in her mind and grew surprisingly fast until it was suddenly the most obvious solution she could have come to. She'd tried pushing Noah away, and it hadn't worked. But what if she tried pulling him closer, instead? He *had* said he didn't do relationships, after all . . . So what scared off a no-strings kind of guy faster than strings? Lots and lots of strings.

She looked toward the floor and tried to funnel all her chaotic emotions into her face.

Sad, sick puppies, she thought. *Poverty. Homelessness. Hungry children.*

She sniffed for good measure.

"Tell me, Pixie," Noah urged.

"I just . . ." she answered, and her voice actually wavered. "I just feel so . . . so stupid!" she blurted, and she wiped a bit of genuine moisture from her eye. Yes! She was crying! She was so proud of herself she could have thrown her hands in the air!

But she didn't. Because that would have ruined the effect.

Noah didn't answer right away, but when she glanced up to gauge his reaction, he looked truly stricken. "I don't understand," he breathed.

"Of course you don't!" she cried, really feeling her part now.

"You said it wouldn't mean anything to you, and I can't believe I thought I could change your mind." Another tear rolled down her cheek, and she watched as his eyes automatically followed it. He didn't say anything, so she pushed harder. "I don't want to be just another notch on your bedpost, or however it is you keep score."

That roused him to action, and he closed his hands around the tops of her arms as if he thought he could press his words into her skin. "I'm not keeping score, Pix!"

"No?"

"No! I'm not that kind of guy!"

"You're not?" she simpered.

"No!" he insisted, his eyes still earnest. "You've got this all wrong, Pixie."

Perfect.

"Oh, Noah!" she gushed. She even managed a convincing hiccup. "I was hoping you'd say that!"

"You were?"

"My parents will love you!" she went on. She draped her arms around his neck and gasped as if she'd just had an epiphany. "What about February?" she asked.

"What?"

"Mom's birthday party is the twenty-fifth, maybe you could come with me! The boys will be there, and my grandparents are making the trip. You could meet them all at once!" she chattered. She lifted up onto her toes and widened her eyes, trying to look as excited as possible.

Noah eyed her like she'd grown a second head and four more arms. "You want me to meet your family? Like . . . next month?"

"Yeah! Why not?" she answered.

He looked her up and down, visibly bewildered. "But we're not even together."

"Well, not yet, but we could always make it official," Olivia said quickly. "You're right, we've basically been on our first date already—really *two* dates if you count the arcade."

His mouth opened slightly, like he was looking for a rebuttal but couldn't find one.

"Besides, you really like me, don't you?" she asked, taking a step farther into his arms.

"Well, yeah, I—"

"Good! Because I really like you, too," she interrupted. She ran her finger along the line of his jaw, pleased to see a rise of color in his cheeks. He was dumbfounded; she could see it in his eyes. "We can do it tonight!" she said, barely keeping the laughter out of her voice. "All my friends are here. Why wait?"

"Uh—"

"Perfect! I'll see you out there! I've got to fix my mascara first," she declared. Then she let her smile spread into a megawatt grin. "I'm so glad you didn't give up!" she added, and then she turned and left the kitchen before she could start laughing. She could practically see Noah's best-laid plans flashing before his eyes.

He'd be gone before dessert.

⚬⚬⚬

"OKAY, SO . . . WHAT was that?" Jake asked the question as he reversed from the parking lot, and Noah slumped against the cushioned seats of his friend's truck and tried to form a reply.

The short answer? He had no idea.

The longer answer? Olivia had lost her mind. Or been body snatched. Or maybe both.

She'd spent the entire party plastered to his side, introducing him to people as her boyfriend and basically acting like her brain had been scrambled somewhere between the kitchen and the living room.

She'd even called him "honey bug."

Twice.

Noah stared through Jake's windshield with blank eyes, barely noticing as the town's landmarks flashed past the windows. Olivia had been more enthusiastic than expected on New Year's Eve. Not that it had slowed him down, but it had surprised him—especially after she'd been so clear about her rules.

Both of which *she'd* broken, by the way.

And then she'd slipped under his arm and fled. She'd left her coat, left her shoes, and left him—still bracing himself against the wall and not totally sure he could move without falling down.

Was it possible it had all meant more to her than he'd realized? He was always up front about his intentions, but occasionally a girl got the wrong impression anyway—though never to quite this extent.

He went over it all again.

Was it *possible*?

No. His common sense spoke up now. *It was not possible.* There was no universe where Olivia Cohen would fawn over him the way she had at dinner—not even if she were having their wedding invitations engraved. In fact, she'd probably bust his chops even harder if she liked him than she did now.

But she doesn't not *like you*, a little voice pointed out.

That was true, too. She couldn't be totally turned off by him and still kiss him the way she had; he didn't think that was possible, either. So, what was he missing? Why was she asking him to come to a family event, calling him cutesy names and using the B-word? Why was she—

His thoughts ground to a halt so fast he almost heard them screech.

She was trying to get rid of him!

Noah smiled as the realization dawned with startling clarity. Oliva Cohen was trying to get rid of him . . . by latching on like a leech. If he weren't on the receiving end of this tactic, he'd have applauded her efforts; for anyone else, it would probably work.

But Noah wouldn't be giving up so easily.

He sat up straight as a sudden sense of excitement filled his chest. "That," he said, turning to Jake, "was desperation. It's like . . ." He searched his memory for what the whole night had reminded him of and finally hit on the right file. "Have you ever seen that Kate Hudson movie where she's trying to scare off Matthew McConaughey by acting like a psychopath?"

"Umm, yeah. But I'm surprised you have."

"My mom likes it," Noah replied, waving Jake's words away. "Anyway, *that's* what Olivia is doing!"

Jake slowed for a red light and flicked his eyes toward his friend. "You know they end up together in that movie, right? Is that the goal here?"

"No," Noah answered quickly. Happily ever after was for fairy tales, and even those could be rewritten. "But she doesn't get to just toss me aside," he went on. "If Olivia wants to pretend we're a happy little couple, then I'm going to call her bluff."

"So, the plan is . . . what, exactly?" Jake asked.

"The plan," Noah said, still putting the pieces together in

his mind, "is to go all-in. Put the chips on the table and force her to show her hand."

"So, you're just going to play chicken and hope she ducks first?"

"Sort of, yeah."

"And what if she doesn't?" Jake asked, his voice skeptical.

Noah huffed, barely even considering the possibility. "Then I'll cross that bridge if I come to it."

"SO, HAVE YOU heard from Noah since the debacle yesterday?" Robin asked from her place on the love seat. She and Kate had spent the night after the party to make the most of their last weekend before homework once again took over all of their lives.

Olivia chuckled and reveled in the sense of victory that surged through her veins. "Nope," she said, letting the word pop from her lips. "And I don't expect to, either. Did you *see* the way his eyes bugged out every time I said the word 'boyfriend'? There is no way he's coming back after that."

"You are *way* too happy about this," Robin said dryly. "Are you sure you really want to scare him off? He seems like a catch."

"Yes, I'm sure," Olivia retorted. "Besides, it's not like we won't wave if we pass each other in the quad or something. He'll just refocus his energy on chasing someone else's tail, and I won't have to worry about it anymore." She settled back against the pile of pillows she'd constructed in front of the couch.

Lexie and Kate came back into the room, both carrying two bowls of early-morning ice cream. "If you're not interested in Noah, why don't you just tell him that outright?" Lexie asked.

Olivia scrunched herself farther into her nest before responding. "I did, and it didn't work," she admitted.

Robin and Kate both burst into laughter.

"But you think this will?" Robin asked.

"Desperate times call for desperate measures!" Olivia declared. "You saw the way he peeled me off him the second Jake suggested they should leave. He couldn't make it to the door fast enough!"

The three other girls shared a skeptical sort of look before Robin crossed her arms stubbornly over her chest. "Methinks the lady doth protest too much," she said, quoting Shakespeare.

Olivia only rolled her eyes and picked up the remote. "Methinks we should just watch the movie," she grumbled, pressing play. There was no reason to dissect the way dinner had gone. Had she been a little over-the-top? Yes. Was it the greatest idea she'd ever had? Probably not. But it had worked, and that was the point. Noah Campbell would find somebody else to annoy and let her finish her semester in peace.

Everybody won. End of story.

About twenty minutes later, Olivia's phone vibrated against the top of the coffee table, the screen glowing brightly in the curtained gloom of the living room. She glanced at it, expecting to see one of her parents' or brothers' names highlighted at the top, but her breath caught in her throat when she saw Noah's name instead.

> **NOAH:** Hey pretty girl! You don't work nights, do you?

She froze, the movie forgotten, as she stared at his question. Another bubble took the first one's place.

> **NOAH:** Some friends of mine are going to play laser tag after class on Tuesday. You want to come? Let me show off my girl? ;)

Olivia had barely finished reading when the device disappeared from the table, and she looked up to find Robin holding it in her hand.

"He wants to *show off his girl?*" she asked, and the glee that crossed her face made Olivia's ribcage tighten.

"He *what?!*" Kate blurted, and Olivia pushed herself off the floor.

"Give that back!" she grunted, swiping at the device.

Robin jumped onto the couch and held it out of arm's reach as she read the message aloud. "Looks like *your boyfriend* got over his shock, Liv," she crowed.

"He's not my boyfriend," Olivia insisted, each word forcing itself out between gritted teeth.

"Well, you stood right here and told him that he is," Kate pointed out. "So now you either have to date him or eat your words."

"I'm not going to date him! He doesn't even *do* relationships!" Olivia cried in dismay, and her own words caused her to pause.

Noah didn't do relationships; he'd told her that himself. So why was he suddenly so chill about being committed? Why was he asking her to meet his friends when he should have been changing his number?

The answer occurred to her all at once, as obvious as the joy on Robin's face.

Noah *knew!* He knew her little performance was a scam, and now he was calling her on it! It was the only thing that made sense!

She clenched her jaw and shook her head as aggravation filled her body. So, he wanted to make this a contest? Fine.

But he hadn't won yet. And he wasn't going to.

"You know what?" she said, stubborn determination taking hold. "I've changed my mind. Looks like I've got a date on Tuesday," she told the group, and Lexie's eyes widened in what looked like dismay.

"You're actually going to do this?" she asked, and Olivia straightened her spine.

"Why not? He doesn't want a relationship any more than I do, so he'll only let it go so far."

Lexie shook her head slowly, as if she couldn't believe what she was hearing. "The poor guy," she murmured. "He won't even know what hit him."

10

"HOW DO I look?" Olivia asked Tuesday night. She put her hands on her hips and turned on the spot for inspection.

"Like Secret Agent Barbie," Lexie replied from her perch on the edge of the bathtub.

Olivia smirked at herself in the mirror and fluffed her high ponytail. It swung jauntily from side to side as she went on to brush unseen dust from her black sweater and jeggings. Most girls on a date wanted to stand out, but on this particular night, Olivia planned to disappear.

She pulled a tube of red lipstick from her makeup bag and smoothed a perfect coat onto her lips before popping them together. "What Noah doesn't know is that Danny, Michael and I practically lived at the laser tag arena near Mom and Dad's house when I was in high school. I'm going to wipe the floor with him."

Lexie snorted. "I thought this was a date. Aren't you supposed to tone it down a little?"

Olivia grinned and reached for the bottle of her signature perfume. "Just think about it, the whole reason for going is to make him regret starting this little game, right? No guy wants to date a girl who shows him up, and to do it in front of his *friends*? Well, he won't be coming back for seconds, that's for sure." She put a spritz of perfume on the inside of one wrist before rubbing it against both sides of her neck.

"I feel like you've said that before," Lexie remarked, and Olivia rolled her eyes at her friend's reflection in the mirror.

"Oh, ye of little faith," she admonished. "Just trust me; I have a plan."

A knock on the door told her Noah had arrived, and she quickly double-checked her pockets for her ID and debit card before heading into the hall.

"I know you have a plan," Lexie called after her. "It's the plan that worries me!"

"I love you, too!" Olivia shouted back. She reached for the doorknob just as Noah knocked again, and she opened the door before he could finish.

"Hey, honey!" she gushed, catching him with his hand still in mid-air. Then she stepped outside and shut the door behind herself. "Ready to go? I can't wait to meet everyone. Do you think they'll like me?"

Noah grinned broadly. "Of course! What's not to like about a beautiful woman?" he asked. Then he slung his arm across her shoulders before guiding her gently toward the stairwell.

Olivia took a long, slow breath and tried to ignore the little sparks of lightning that pricked through the fabric of her shirt. She couldn't shrug him off if he was supposed to be her "boyfriend"; he had certain permissions now that went with the title, and she was going to have to give a little.

Well, that or admit she'd been lying through her teeth before . . . and that wasn't going to happen.

"Now, there will be eight of us—you, me and six of the guys," he explained as they descended to the parking lot. "The arena just opened last semester. Apparently, some rich alum took pity on us poor Cypress Valley kids with nothing to do around here."

He spent the trip across town explaining every minute detail of the game as if the words "laser tag" weren't mostly common sense, and Olivia did her best to act like she was listening intently and not like she was contemplating taping his mouth shut. Finally, they pulled into the parking lot of a massive building just outside the city limits. There were cars everywhere, even in places that shouldn't technically have been parking spaces, and she started to wonder how they were even going to get in.

"You reserve a game time," Noah explained, obviously seeing the question on her face. "Ours starts in fifteen minutes; the guys should already be here." He got out of the car and came around to open her door, though she beat him to the punch purely by force of habit.

His hand warmed the small of her back as he guided her through the lobby doors and then toward a small group of college guys who stood clustered near the equipment counter.

"Pixie, meet Parker, Beckett, Randall, Don, Carson and Rock," Noah said rapidly, pointing to each of his friends in turn.

"Rock?" she repeated.

A guy with red hair and freckles gave a sheepish wave. "It's Rick, actually," he explained.

"But he misspelled his own name on a biology final once, so he doesn't deserve to keep it," a blond interjected, stepping forward. "I'm Beckett. And you're . . . Pixie?"

"Olivia," she corrected as she shook the hand he offered. "Pixie is kind of an inside joke."

"Got it, got it," Beckett replied. He bobbed his head as he spoke. "Well, it's about time to suit up. Everybody ready?"

There was a general murmur of consent from the group, and they moved as one toward the counter to retrieve their vests and guns. Noah grabbed two vests from a pile and set the larger one on the ground before turning to drape the other over Olivia's head.

"So, remember what I said in the car? We're playing free-for-all first—every man for himself, unlimited hits. Then we'll play capture the flag with our team at the end. Sound good?"

Olivia nodded, already feeling adrenaline surge through her veins. "Sounds great," she replied.

Noah snapped a buckle on each side of her hips and then yanked on a strap to tighten the armor to her torso. The sudden change of momentum caused Olivia to stumble forward, and she caught herself with both hands against his chest.

She closed her grip around a fistful of his work shirt, tugging him impossibly closer, and he made a sound that seemed like approval. Then he angled her head back with both hands, deepening the kiss even more, and she felt her knees turn to jelly. Her hands took on lives of their own, going everywhere and nowhere all at once, and he made another noise when her palms found bare skin beneath his shirt. She vaguely knew she was breaking one of her own rules, but she didn't care. She felt inexplicably greedy—like maybe she'd been starving all this time and hadn't known it.

The only clear thought in her mind was that she didn't want him to stop.

"Steady now," he said, and Olivia blinked to find Noah's full, *present-day* attention fixed on her. There was amusement in his eyes now, but if she focused hard enough, she could still imagine the heat that had been there on New Year's Eve.

Except . . . she wasn't imagining it. He raised one hand and tucked a wayward strand of hair behind her ear, and she felt something stutter traitorously inside her chest.

Stop it! she told herself. *He's playing a game, remember?*

Fortunately, a buzzer sounded somewhere overhead, and a deep, electronic voice announced a two-minute warning before the next game.

Noah ducked down and grabbed his vest from the floor before strapping it on, seemingly unaffected by whatever moment they'd just had. He snatched her hand in his. "Come on," he urged. "This will be fun."

A doorway with red lights around the frame revealed the arena beyond, and Olivia remembered why she was there as their group followed about a dozen other players inside. The guys ahead of them quickly dispersed, and she did a cursory scan of her surroundings as her eyes adjusted. The arena was set up like an old warehouse, with barrels and barriers of all types outlined in eerie fluorescent piping. The balcony of an upper level glowed orange above her head, but she didn't see any obvious way to access it. Finding one would be objective number two.

Objective number one was still holding her hand.

"This way," he whispered, and he took her with him toward what turned out to be an alcove, partially concealed by a stack of wooden crates.

"One minute!" the computerized voice warned.

Noah pulled her into a crouch behind their barricade. "You nervous, Pix?" he asked.

Olivia merely hummed in response, which he obviously took as confirmation.

"Don't worry. I'll protect you," he assured her with a cocky smile.

She exhaled slowly, and her index finger tensed near the trigger of her gun. She was here for one reason and one reason only—and it *wasn't* to play damsel in distress. "What happened to 'every man for himself'?" she asked.

Noah shrugged—a motion she could only see because the dimly-lit sensors on his shoulders moved up and down. "I know, but I can make an exception."

"Aww! Thanks, honey bug," she cooed.

There was no indication he even knew she had tilted her gun up from her hip. The lights in the arena flashed once, twice . . .

"Get ready," he told her, and the starting buzzer echoed in her ears.

The next sound was the firing of her weapon, and the sensors on his vest lit up like the Fourth of July.

"Don't worry. I am," she replied.

"What the—?"

But Olivia didn't stick around to answer. She was already running through the dark.

❧

"ALL HAIL THE warrior princess!" Parker shouted as he burst through the arena's exterior doors and out into the chilly evening air. The rest of the guys echoed his words, and Noah bit the inside of his cheek to keep from joining in.

He'd made a mistake. Several, actually.

First, he'd underestimated his opponent. He'd honestly expected Olivia to turn his invitation down flat the way she'd done before, but she was clearly more dedicated to the cause than he'd realized. Second, he'd given her an audience—one that was now eating out of her hand.

"Aww, come on, Campbell," Beckett said, knocking his shoulder against Noah's as they walked. "Why the long face? It's not like she held you to your lowest score in memorable history. Or hunted you like an animal. Or made you her personal whipping boy. Oh, wait, she did!"

Laughter burst from the group as its members made their way down the sidewalk toward a burger joint nearby.

Noah glanced toward Olivia where she walked beside him. He was sure if he looked up the word "smug" in the dictionary, he'd find her current expression sketched in the margins. She'd obviously abandoned the doe-eyed damsel routine, for which he was grateful, but she'd made a few mistakes, too—the biggest of which was assuming her total domination would be a turnoff when in fact it was strangely the opposite. He clenched his jaw and made a conscious effort not to dwell on the fact that Olivia in laser tag gear bore a striking resemblance to Lara Croft in *Tomb Raider.*

"Liv, are you coming?" Carson shouted from up ahead, and Olivia's pace increased.

She turned around and walked backwards several yards ahead of Noah. "Come on, Campbell! Try to keep up with the big boys!" she taunted, and her ponytail bounced with every step.

Noah narrowed his eyes and refused to let her goad him. She may have won this battle, but the war wasn't over.

He just needed to raise the stakes.

THE NEXT AFTERNOON, Noah loitered near a water fountain across the hall from the Department of Social Work while he waited for a good opening. Some professor with a pair of yellow pencils stuck into her bird's nest bun was on her cell phone right in front of the desk where a cute blonde student assistant was pretending to write something down.

He knew she was pretending because she'd actually been watching him for the last five minutes. She glanced up again, and he gave her a practiced smile, one he knew made girls blush and fidget. After all, what was the point of being pretty if you couldn't use it to your advantage from time to time?

Finally, the professor finished her call and wandered away, leaving the coast clear. Noah pushed off the wall and quickly approached the office door—a man on a mission. "Hi," he said, stepping up to the desk. "I'm Noah."

The young woman—obviously another student worker—chewed on her lower lip. "Hi, Noah. I'm Bethany. What can I do for you?"

"Well," he started, leaning his hands against the top of her desk. "I'm hoping you can help me with something. You see, I need information, and I'm pretty sure you have it."

"Oh, yeah?"

"Yeah. I'm looking for someone—a senior social work student, a friend of mine—and I need to know where he might be on, say, a Thursday."

A coy smile stretched across Bethany's face. "You can't just ask him?" she asked.

Noah smiled back. "If I did that, I wouldn't have a reason to talk to you, now would I?"

A bright pink blush rose in her cheeks. "Well, senior students work their internships Monday through Thursday, so your friend won't have a campus class until Friday afternoon," she replied. "Then they're all in capstone at two thirty."

"See there? You *did* have what I needed," Noah answered. "Where is that class?"

Bethany nodded toward the hall. "You were standing in front of it."

"Oh, so right where I saw you? That'll be easy to remember." He winked, and she beamed up at him from her seat as he straightened. "Thanks, Bethany. Maybe I'll be back around sometime."

"I'll be here," she replied as he took a few backward steps toward the door. He gave her another smile before turning and making his way down the hall. Friday was only two days away.

Good thing he had a few favors to cash in.

11

OLIVIA JUMPED AS her friend Clara elbowed her in the ribs. "Samson's talking about intern evaluations," she whispered. "Act like you're paying attention."

"Thanks," Olivia replied. "I got distracted."

"Obviously. You look like your hamster fell off the wheel."

Olivia let out a tired sigh and tried to focus on her professor's words. Her hamster was running alright, just on a completely different track. This class was supposed to help graduating seniors take the final steps between their internships and the real world, but Olivia was starting to wonder if she'd ever really be ready. She'd only been working at the Harrelson Center for Children's Services for two weeks, and already she'd seen more of the "real world" than she'd been prepared for.

In the last four days alone, she'd been on two child-removal calls—one of which required police intervention—and observed one ugly meeting between a set of parents, a case worker and the district attorney. But she'd also been privileged to see a little boy go home with his forever family, and then she'd helped plan a teenager's first-ever birthday party. Olivia knew she'd never forget the look on the girl's face when she'd realized the setup was for her.

The career field she'd chosen would definitely have its ups and downs . . . She just hoped she could handle all of them.

"If you've applied to graduate school, you should be hearing from them by the end of next month," Dr. Samson said, but her thought was cut short by a knock at the door. The confused professor left her podium to answer it, and Olivia felt the attention level in the hall rise like the tide. There was a moment of hushed conversation by the door—during which it seemed as if Dr. Samson would deny the visitor entry—but then she relented.

"Students, it seems we'll have a *brief* intermission," she said, emphasizing the word *brief*, "in the name of love."

"In the name of *what*?" Clara whispered, but Olivia only shrugged in confusion. She didn't know anything more than the next person.

The whole class watched as four young men in matching navy sport coats entered the room in single file. One was carrying a small speaker, which he set on the now-empty podium. Dr. Samson waited with her shoulder propped against the wall and her brows arched, clearly as mystified as the rest of the room.

"Is Olivia Cohen in here?" the guy with the speaker asked, and Olivia felt her blood run cold. Clara swiveled in her seat and leaned back, her face alight with a thousand silent questions. Olivia gave her friend the tiniest silent shake of her head and hoped she would get the message.

No. Please, no.

"Olivia?" the guy asked again, and when Olivia made no motion to answer, Clara's hand shot into the air.

"She's up here!" she called.

Olivia turned to her friend with fire in her eyes. "Traitor!" she hissed through clenched teeth.

Clara grinned broadly, practically bouncing in her seat. "Oh, come on! Let me live vicariously!" she begged.

Olivia thought of a few retorts, but it was too late to give them. Three of the intruders were already climbing the lecture hall stairs, and a familiar beat was coming from the speaker down below. The quartet started to snap their fingers in time.

What was happening?!

The closest man, obviously the ringleader of this little band, broke into the opening line of "My Girl" by The Temptations just as he reached Olivia's row. Olivia felt her entire body gain a thousand pounds and do its best to sink through the bottom of her chair. Of all the days in the year to find an aisle seat!

The song went on, all four boys now staggered along the stairs beside her as they harmonized on the chorus, and many of Olivia's classmates seemed to have joined in as well. At least, the sound had grown exponentially louder since the first verse—though that might have just been the blood pounding in her ears.

Clara latched both hands onto her arm. "You should see your face!" she said gleefully, but Olivia didn't have to *see* her face. She could *feel* it, every single inch, as her skin seemed to vibrate of its own accord. What in the world—

Her confusion was put to rest as the song ended. The room broke into applause and cheers, and one of the singers laid a blank white notecard on the tabletop in front of her. At least, the side facing up was blank, but when she snatched it and turned it over, the opposite side sported a single sentence in cramped print.

"All hail my warrior princess."

Olivia felt her blood pressure rise even further, and her fingers actually shook.

Noah. Campbell.

He didn't know when to give up, did he?

She crumpled the card in her hand and stuffed it into her backpack. If he wanted a fight, then he'd get one.

And he'd regret it.

TWO DAYS LATER, Olivia put her car in park in front of Watson's Grocery Store and flipped down the visor mirror to double-check her reflection. Then, she rolled her shoulders back and tried to remember every word her high school theatre teacher had ever said.

Own the room. Feel your character. Play to the audience.

She let out a long, calming sigh and craned her neck to peer through her windshield and into the front store windows. There he was, stacking what looked like boxes of canned soda near the registers. The store seemed fairly quiet for the moment, though there were customers in two checkout lanes and a small cluster of people in employee uniforms loitering around the service desk.

Perfect.

Olivia grabbed a small, insulated bag from her passenger's seat and took it with her as she climbed from the car and started her march toward the store. The click of her heels on the pavement provided a background beat for the swing of her hips, and she tried to imagine she was on some kind of fashion runway.

One that led straight past a large advertisement for cocktail sauce . . . but no matter.

The automatic doors whooshed open, and she strode inside, head held high, with the world's biggest smile on her face. "Oh, sweetheart!" she called, her voice loud and clear in the half-empty store. A dozen heads swung her way, but she stayed focused on her target, who hadn't looked up from the display he was creating.

"Honey bug!" she called again. "There you are! I almost called the front desk!"

Noah finally turned as she came to a stop beside him, having evidently realized someone was talking to him. His brow furrowed in confusion, and he opened his mouth to respond, but she didn't let him.

"You forgot your medicine, sweetie, so I brought it up to you. Oh! And another pair of briefs, just like you asked, though the silk may have gotten cold in the bag. Maybe that'll help, though."

There were a few audible snickers from nearby, and Olivia had to work to keep a straight face. She shoved the thermal pouch into Noah's hands and barreled on, making sure he wouldn't be able to get a word in edgewise. "The *special cream*"—she whispered these words as loudly as she could—"is in the side pocket, just in case. I know how many burritos you had for lunch; those are gonna burn on the way out."

Someone from behind the service desk hooted out loud, and Noah clamped his mouth shut as a visible flush climbed into his ears. Olivia patted the side of his face the way her grandmother used to do to her brothers. "Don't be embarrassed, honey bug. Good colon health is very important!" She winked to drive the point home. "Toodle-oo!" she sang, and then she turned on her heel and waltzed back toward the door as if their enlightening little conversation were as normal as snowflakes in the winter.

A wave of laughter from Noah's coworkers followed her through the doors, and when she'd crossed the lobby, she finally looked back and saw him clutching the thermal bag to his chest as three of his coworkers tried to take it from him—probably to find out whether or not there was really a pair of silk briefs inside.

They wouldn't be disappointed—she'd picked a pair with pink Hawaiian flowers on every inch.

Noah glanced toward the doors as she backed through the second set, and she held her hands up in a heart shape against her chest. Noah narrowed his eyes, the only indication he'd seen her gesture at all, and Olivia threw her head back and laughed all the way to her car.

Game. Set. Match.

"I TOLD YOU this was a bad idea," Jake said from his place at the kitchen table. "Olivia is a force to be reckoned with, and you, my friend, have woken the beast."

Conner, on the other hand, said nothing. He was laughing too hard to speak.

Noah didn't blame him. If the whole incident had happened to anyone else, he would have done the same thing—but, as it was, he'd been too busy fending off questions about his "colon health" all night to truly appreciate the evil genius of Olivia's performance. "It isn't over yet," he replied. He turned and resumed pacing between the kitchen sink and the living room couch. "Noah Campbell doesn't give up on a challenge. Noah Campbell is here to win! Noah Campbell—"

"—talks about himself in the third person," Conner wheezed,

having apparently collected himself enough to form intelligent words again.

Noah glared at him and kept talking. "—is *also* a force to be reckoned with, and that little minx hasn't seen anything yet. It's been fun and games until now, but the gloves are coming off. I'm gonna show her who she's dealing with. I'm gonna—"

He stopped abruptly and stared at a pine knot on the bathroom door as an idea came together in his mind. "I'm gonna sweep her off her feet," he finished, and he turned to see Jake scrutinizing him with a spoonful of cereal paused halfway to his mouth.

"Meaning?" his friend asked warily.

"Meaning I'm going full boyfriend mode. Do you know what day it is?"

"Sunday?"

"Sunday, February 12," Noah answered, emphasizing each word in turn. "Do you know what that means?"

"That you can read a calendar?" Conner asked.

"No! It means February 14—aka *Valentine's Day*—is in forty-eight hours!"

Conner's face went blank, as if he were truly concerned for his roommate's sanity at this point. "Dude, Valentine's Day is dangerous. This is when you hunker down! Grab a shift at work, avoid eye contact with women, curl into a ball and hope for the best."

"No," Noah said, a maniacal sort of laughter rising in his chest. "Valentine's Day is perfect!"

"WHAT ARE YOU doing for Valentine's Day?" Robin asked abruptly, and Olivia surfaced from her thoughts with a distracted sort of static buzzing around her ears.

"What?"

"I asked what you're doing for Valentine's Day," Robin repeated. "You know, now that you have a boyfriend, or whatever you think he is."

Valentine's Day . . .

"I don't know, when is it?" Olivia asked. Then she dipped one of her onion rings into a puddle of ketchup.

"Tuesday," Robin answered.

"Tuesday?"

"Yeah, like *this* Tuesday. The day after tomorrow? Forty-eight hours from now?"

The gears in Olivia's mind started to spin. She hadn't even realized Valentine's Day was that week. She normally didn't care, and Noah hadn't said anything.

Noah hasn't said anything!

Olivia felt her cheeks stretch into a slow grin. "Robin, you're a genius!"

"I know," her friend replied blithely. Then she paused and met Olivia's eye. "Why?"

"Because it's Valentine's Day! Girlfriends care about Valentine's Day, and he's got a girlfriend now. He hasn't said a thing! I bet it hasn't even crossed his mind! Tuesday will get here, absolutely nothing will happen, and then I'll have logical grounds to go all high-maintenance basket case on him, and that'll be the end!"

Robin eyed her skeptically as a waitress came to refill their sodas. "I don't think that word means what you think it means," she said when the woman was gone.

Olivia only huffed good-naturedly, her mood dramatically improved. "Don't *Princess Bride* me. It'll work this time," she said.

Robin took a long slurp of her soda and gave a knowing sort of smile. "Whatever you say, my dear. Whatever you say."

12

"DO YOU HAVE a meat thermometer? I think that's the only thing I forgot," Noah asked as Lexie made her way to the kitchen door that Tuesday evening.

"Yeah, in that utensil drawer on your left," she replied.

Noah yanked the drawer open and rummaged until he found what he needed. "Perfect, thanks."

Lexie stood just on the edge of his peripheral vision, and he glanced over to see if she had any final instructions before she left for her own romantic evening. The expression on her face was one he couldn't quite read.

"You're not going to hurt her, are you?" she asked at last. "Because if you do, I'll have to cut off your head; that's what she would do for me."

Noah chuckled and opened the oven door to baste the pork tenderloin again. The smell of soy sauce, garlic and thyme hit him square in the face, and his mouth watered; he hadn't cooked anything this good in a long time. "Don't worry, Lex," he said.

"Okay," she replied, though she still seemed unsure. "Because

I really don't understand whatever this is, and I don't want to be the cause of—"

Noah shut the oven and reached over to lay a hand on her shoulder. "Lexie, really. It's just dinner," he assured her. "All you did was let me inside."

She pursed her lips and grunted as she turned toward the hall. "Pretty fancy dinner . . . on Valentine's Day," she mumbled, and Noah watched as she moved out of sight. "Don't make me regret this!" she called from the living room. "I'll sic Jacob on you."

Noah snorted and went back to slicing shallots on a bright-blue cutting board. "It'll be fine, Lexie!" he called, but he wasn't sure she'd heard before the front door shut behind her. "Besides," he muttered to himself, "I could take Jake any day."

Forty-five minutes passed while he cooked in silence, the sounds of his own utensils the only things to be heard. In addition to the tenderloin, the evening's menu also included white-cheddar scalloped potatoes, steamed garlic beans and some cherry custard tarts he'd made ahead of time. He was particularly proud of those, since he'd never been good at desserts, but Olivia had a sweet tooth, and he was leaving no stone unturned.

"Besides, women like men who can cook," he heard his mother say, and he let a smile spread across his face; "Operation End Game" would finally put that theory to the test. He hummed to himself as he pulled the meat from the oven and set it out to rest on the counter. His watch read 5:15 p.m., and according to Lexie, that meant Olivia should be pulling into the parking lot shortly. He went to set the table, tweaking an arrangement of pink roses while he was at it, then lit the tall, white tapers he'd found in a drawer at his house. He pressed a button on a small speaker, and soft jazz music filled the quiet space.

He was going to win this thing tonight, even if he had to bend over backwards to do it.

OLIVIA PAUSED JUST outside the door of her apartment and took a deep, grounding breath. Today had been a first in a lot of ways—and none of them good.

"Try not to take it home with you," her friend Monica had advised, but that was easier said than done. Here Olivia was, at home, and she could still feel the ugliness of the day plastered across her skin. She wondered if it would ever wash off.

She exhaled again and pushed the door open—but that was as far as she got. Instead of a mercifully empty apartment, she found herself staring at Noah Campbell, who was standing beside her dining table in a dress shirt and dark jeans. It took several moments and a quick glance at the number on the door to assure herself that she was, in fact, walking into the correct apartment.

Her eyes skated across the table itself, which was covered in a cloth for probably the first time ever and set beautifully with real plates and silverware, three flickering candles and a vase of vibrant flowers. She sighed without meaning to. She did *not* have the energy for this tonight.

"Happy Valentine's Day," Noah said smoothly. He looked like a cat who'd just cornered a mouse. "I hope you like surprises."

Valentine's Day. She'd completely forgotten.

The look on her face must have been more than he'd bargained for, because his tone changed from one of false innocence to real concern.

"Pixie, what's wrong?" he asked. "I was going for speechless, but you look like your light has gone out."

Olivia dragged herself across the threshold at last and leaned back against the door to shut it behind her. Then she looked around the room again, her eyes landing on the serving dishes laden with food. All of this was more than she could handle when what she really wanted was to crawl beneath a dark blanket and never come out. "You cooked," she said blankly. "And brought flowers."

Noah looked down at the table and waved a flippant hand through the air. "Yeah, but . . . just . . . ignore that." He turned off the music before taking her hand and tugging her toward the first open chair. She sank into it as if her whole body weighed more than it ever had before.

Noah turned a second chair until it was right in front of hers, and then he sat down as well and leaned forward. "What is it Peter Pan says? 'Clap if you believe in fairies'?" he asked. He clapped his hands, his expression earnest, and Olivia felt the start of a smile despite herself.

"Funny. You *would* be the boy who never grows up," she said.

The worry returned to Noah's face as he reached out and took her hands in his, first one and then, hesitantly, the other. "What is it, Pix? You can tell me."

Olivia met his eyes and let out another long, tired sigh. There was part of her that wanted to unpack everything—maybe then she could stop carrying it like a rock inside her heart—but it wasn't her story to share.

"No, I can't," she whispered, shaking her head. "I can't tell anybody."

"Okay. Then tell me how you feel about it."

Olivia closed her eyes and tried to distance herself from the words she'd heard and the mental images they'd painted. She tried to see the forensic interview from somewhere near the ceiling, as if she hadn't been part of it at all. She could see herself on her stool in the corner while the little girl told an investigator her story—while the horrors of an eight-year-old's life became words on paper, evidence in a file that would define her forever.

Not that reality hadn't already done that.

"I think I've made a huge mistake," she finally said, the words sneaking past all her defenses. She opened her eyes and stared down at the floor between Noah's feet. "I don't think I'm cut out for this job after all."

She could feel Noah's attention on her face, even though she couldn't see it.

"Why not?" he asked.

"Because I can't do it!" she snapped, whipping her gaze up to his. His face shimmered through an unwelcome layer of tears, and she willed them back to where they came from. "How am I supposed to help these kids if I can't even keep myself together? If I can't handle hearing what they've been through?" she asked. "It's impossible! There is so much evil in the world, and I'm just one person. What good will I ever do?"

There was silence, and Olivia watched a tiny bead of hot wax slide slowly down the side of one of the white candles. She was starting to wish she hadn't said anything when Noah finally moved. One of his hands slipped out of hers, and he hooked a finger beneath her chin and turned her head so she was looking up at him.

"You're allowed to feel things, Pix. If you didn't, you'd be no good to anyone," he said. "And you're right, you can't save them all . . . but maybe you can save one, or two, or five, or twenty. There are kids in this world who are praying to find you, Pixie. The only way you'll let them down is if you aren't there."

Olivia watched Noah's mouth move as he spoke, as if she needed proof the words were actually coming from him. A surge of new emotion welled up in her chest. "Since when are you so smart?" she asked, trying and failing to make a joke.

"I'm not actually an idiot, Pixie; I just play one on TV," he replied, and Olivia felt a wobbly smile stretch across her face.

His thumb moved along the crest of her cheek, and she felt the moisture of a tear she hadn't known had fallen. She jerked her head away and scrubbed both palms over her face, unwilling to become one of those girls who let pretty boys dry their eyes. "Thanks, Noah," she murmured.

He straightened in his seat, regarding her with a new kind of look that made her feel like he could see everything she'd ever tried to hide about herself. "Anytime, Olivia."

Something about her name sounded odd coming from his mouth, and Olivia realized all at once that he'd never used it before. Hearing it now was both deeply unsettling and profoundly reassuring, all at the same time. It was a paradox she didn't have the strength to contemplate just then.

There was a moment of silence, and then he released her hand abruptly. "Alright, new plan," he announced. "Go change." He pressed both palms flat on his thighs and rose to stand.

"What?" Olivia asked, confused.

Noah cupped his hand behind each of the three candles in turn and blew out their flickering flames. "You heard me. Go change, the more comfortable the better. If you have bunny slippers, I won't judge." He crossed the dim living room and flipped on both the table lamps, flooding the space with light. "I'll make you a plate."

His tone left no room for argument, and Olivia felt her body sag with relief. He wasn't going to make her go through with whatever he'd set up for the night—which was surprising, given his clear advantage. She'd been ready to fold the second she walked in the door.

She rose woodenly to her feet and made a beeline for her bedroom on autopilot. Several minutes later, she opened the door again and found Noah standing beside the now-clear dining room table, his hands shoved awkwardly into his pockets. It was one of the first times—or, maybe the *only* time—she'd ever seen him look uncertain, and it was oddly adorable.

"I put away the leftovers, but if you want more you can just reheat. There's dessert in the fridge," he explained, and Olivia glanced at the low coffee table, where there was only one dinner plate prepared.

"You're leaving?"

Noah stopped, his brow pinched a bit in the middle. "Well, I just figured you'd want me to go," he replied.

Olivia looked again at the single plate and then around the lonely living room, and she suddenly realized she didn't actually want to be alone. "Could you stay?" she asked, her voice smaller than she'd like. There was no telling when Lexie would get back, and somebody was better than nobody, right?

Noah considered her for a minute, almost like he was weighing the pros and cons, before raising one shoulder in an almost-casual shrug. "Alright. If you want," he said. Then he ducked down the hallway toward the kitchen. Olivia heard the refrigerator door open and the clink of dishes while she settled herself on the couch, and he returned with a second loaded plate a few minutes later.

"So, what'll it be?" he asked, already making himself comfortable beside her. "*Parks and Rec? Sons of Anarchy?*"

Olivia shook her head and picked up the remote. "Nope," she replied. She turned on the DVR and pulled up the replay of the previous night's episode of *The Bachelor*, which she'd missed.

Noah tilted his head back against the top of the couch. "You've got to be kidding," he groaned, and Olivia felt an evil sort of pleasure expand inside her chest like a balloon.

"You asked," she responded.

He wiped one hand down his face in resignation and sat up before pulling his plate into his lap. Olivia left hers on the table. It smelled good, even from there, and she knew logically that she should eat something, but she just couldn't summon the desire for food. All she really wanted was to sit on this couch and turn her brain to mush with the world's stupidest reality television. Honestly, the only reason she watched was so she could remind Robin how ridiculous the whole thing was.

Well, that and the cat fights. Everybody loved those.

"What's with his shirt?" Noah asked, referring to Ben, the current Bachelor himself, who'd arrived in Belize in a private helicopter. Olivia shrugged; she'd grown used to Ben's penchant for deep-V necklines by this point in the season.

"I think he lost the rest of it," she said. Half the words were drowned by a yawn, and she leaned to one side without really thinking. Her cheek landed squarely on Noah's upper arm.

You should probably get up, a small voice admonished, but she was too tired to listen. She felt like she could crawl into bed and sleep for a week.

HOURS LATER, OLIVIA woke with a start. The living room was half lit by only one table lamp, and the rest of the apartment felt and sounded empty. She raised her head from the small pillow she'd been sleeping on and realized she didn't remember lying down. Or covering herself with a blanket. She sat up further and looked around the room, dragging a hand through her hair. Her gaze caught on a vase of pink roses on the dining room table, and the rest of the evening flooded back all at once.

Noah.

Dinner. Flowers. Candles.

The Bachelor.

She pushed off the soft throw blanket and swung her feet to the floor. "Noah?" she called, but all she got in response was silence. Then she padded down the hall to Lexie's room and found it empty as well.

Olivia returned to where she'd started and stood in the middle of the living room with her hands on her hips, not quite sure what to do with herself. Then, she saw a yellow square tucked beneath the flowers—a sheet from the Post-it pad on the fridge. She lifted the vase and pulled the adhesive from the table.

I don't like Courtney, the first line said, and a smile grew across Olivia's face. So, Noah had at least stayed long enough to meet all six candidates for Ben's final rose. *But I do believe in fairies*, the note finished, and something hot pricked the corners of Olivia's eyes.

Apparently, Noah Campbell could have his moments of redemption.

THE NEXT NIGHT, Noah sat in his car outside Watson's Grocery Store and polished off a turkey sandwich from the deli case. It had seemed like enough ten minutes ago, but now he was wishing he had the pork from Olivia's house. Too bad he'd left it all in her fridge; it was probably one of the most delicious meals he'd ever made.

And she hadn't even touched it—at least, not while he was there.

He twirled his phone where it lay on the center console and resisted the urge to check it again. He'd texted her twice that morning without response, which didn't necessarily surprise him. He wasn't stupid—he knew she had plenty of other friends to turn to if she needed something; she'd only kept him around last night because he was available. He doubted she'd spent any real time thinking about it afterward.

He, on the other hand, couldn't seem to *stop* thinking about it—which didn't make any sense, since the only reason he'd been present at all was because of their little game. And it wasn't like he'd never had dinner and watched TV with a girl before.

But, if he were being honest, it wasn't what had happened that made his insides squirm like a bag of cats. It was what *hadn't*.

He *hadn't* felt the walls closing in on him when she'd snuggled close. He *hadn't* concocted a reason to leave early. He *hadn't* even pretended to visit the bathroom to gain some space. He'd just . . . stayed. He'd let her fall asleep against his shoulder like it had happened a thousand times, and then he'd laid her down and tucked her in when the show was over and locked the door behind him when he left.

It's just biology, he assured himself. *She was upset, which stressed me out and raised my cortisol levels. Close proximity created oxytocin, which activated my parasympathetic nervous system and overrode the fight-or-flight response I normally have when girls want to cuddle. Simple science.*

A soft tap at his driver's side window interrupted his train of thought, and he looked over to find Olivia—of all people—standing outside the car. His window didn't work, so he popped open the door to talk to her.

"Hey," he said, furrowing his brow. "What are you doing here?"

Olivia shrugged. "We needed more strawberry oatmeal, and the Walmart in Cypress Valley is out," she said. Then she held out a small, insulated cooler bag. "I brought you some leftovers in case you got a dinner break."

Noah looked warily toward the bag without taking it. "This feels very familiar," he declared.

She smiled slightly. "Don't worry," she assured him. "It's just food. Really good food, actually; who knew you were such a good cook?"

She sounded surprised and—unless he was imagining it—more than a little impressed. He brushed the comment off as if it didn't matter, even though it ignited a spark of pride within his chest. "I have many hidden talents," he said, accepting the bag at last. "I'm glad you got to try some. You didn't have to share."

"It's nothing," she answered with a wave of her hand. "Like I said, I needed to come up anyway. I just wanted to say thank you—for the dinner, and for hanging out with me. It was nice to not be alone."

"No problem." Noah unzipped the top of the bag and immediately smelled soy sauce and garlic from the meat. The container was still warm, and his stomach growled loudly, despite the fact that he'd just finished eating.

"Well, I'll let you enjoy. You probably don't have a lot of time left," Olivia said as she took a step backward. "Thank you, again."

She didn't stay to let him answer, and Noah peeled back the top of the covered dish without wasting any more time. Then he realized he didn't have any utensils. He reached into the bag again, hoping she'd thought to bring him a fork, and was surprised to discover not only a fork but another square container as well. He pulled it out and opened it.

Inside was another sandwich. A toasted sandwich, to be exact . . . with dark-brown Nutella and pale bananas visible along the edges.

"My comfort food is Nutella toast with bananas."

She'd remembered!

He looked up, first toward the store and then around the parking lot, and saw Olivia already climbing back into her Mustang in the next row, her hands empty except for her purse.

He smiled.

She hadn't bought oatmeal.

13

ON MONDAY AFTERNOON, Noah left the grocery store and looked this way and that across the sparsely populated parking lot. His shoulders slumped when he realized there were no blue pickup trucks anywhere—not that he'd expected curbside taxi service, but he'd at least been hoping Jake wouldn't forget about him.

He pulled his phone from his pocket before dialing his best friend's number; it was one of the few he actually had memorized. The line rang, and rang, and rang again before finally connecting, but what he heard wasn't Jake's voice at all.

"Noah?" a woman asked, and it took a few seconds for him to realize he was talking to Lexie.

"Hey," he answered. "Where's Jake?"

"We're in Copper Hill with his family. Did you need something?"

"Yeah, he's supposed to pick me up from work. Conner hid all my tires, and my car is up on blocks in our driveway."

"Noah, I'm sorry. Jake's great-grandmother passed away a few hours ago, and the whole family is really busy."

"Oh, tell him I'm sorry," Noah answered, feeling his chest deflate. His conscience warred between feeling sorry that his friend had lost someone—which obviously wasn't Jake's fault—and irked by the very real possibility that he'd have to walk home.

"Do you have any coworkers going that way?" Lexie asked.

Noah glanced through the front windows of the store and saw Riley talking to a customer and Brendon cleaning up broken glass from a jar of spaghetti sauce. "No, not for a while anyway. I got lucky with a short shift," he answered. "But don't worry about it. You go take care of Jake, and I'll figure something out."

"You should ask Olivia," Lexie suggested.

Noah considered this for a moment. He knew Olivia would be at her internship right now. But all he knew about it was that it involved working with kids; he honestly had no idea where it was actually located.

"She's right down the street at the Harrelson Center. You know that place with the purple sign?" Lexie explained.

Noah leaned forward to peer down the four-lane highway in front of the store. He remembered seeing a big purple sign with stick figures and rainbows on it a few blocks away, though he'd never paid much attention. He could almost see it through the trees from where he stood.

"You probably should have thought of her first," Lexie added. "You know . . . since you're dating and all."

There was a taunting edge to her voice that reminded Noah why this option made perfect sense. Or, at least, why it *would*—if he and Olivia were actually together.

"You're right," he said. "I can't believe I didn't!"

Lexie said goodbye and was gone, and the cell phone turned into a paperweight in Noah's hand. He looked down the road again. On Valentine's Day, Lexie had told him Olivia would leave work at five. He glanced at his watch; it was still only four forty. With no other immediate options, he began picking his way through the parking lots and hedgerows that divided the businesses on this side of the highway. Then he sprinted across the four-lane directly into the driveway of something called the Harrelson Center for Children's Services. A parking lot to the left sported a "staff only" sign, and he followed the curb where it curved in that direction. To his relief, Olivia's purple Mustang came into view a few moments later; he took up a comfortable position against the trunk of the car and prepared to wait.

Just after five, the back door of the building finally opened, and people began to file out, some climbing into the cars around him with brief and curious glances in his direction. He nodded politely to several older ladies and greeted a gentleman with a deferential "evening, sir" before the sound of young laughter met his ears. A cluster of college-aged girls was exiting the building, and he caught sight of Olivia among them. She turned away from her friends and started across the lot, though she stopped on the sidewalk when her eyes met his. Surprise and confusion flooded her face, and she looked to either side as if preparing to be ambushed.

"Hi," she said. "What are you doing here?"

"Surprising my girl at work." He flashed her a winning smile, just in case it would help his cause.

She looked around again as she came closer. "Surprising her with *what*?"

Noah almost laughed. "So suspicious! Can't I do something without an ulterior motive?"

"Not usually."

He sighed dramatically and slipped around the edge of her fender to intercept her. "Well, that's unfortunate, because I'm just here to ask how your day has been."

She looked up, still clearly unconvinced, and Noah cleared his throat.

"Alright, I'm here to beg," he admitted, and a new light dawned in her eyes.

"To beg? Well, it's about time," she replied. "What exactly are you begging *for?*"

"A ride home with a pretty girl."

One of Olivia's eyebrows popped up, and a devilish sort of smirk spread across her face. "Well, then it's too bad for you that I'm not going straight home."

"I'll go anywhere you go—to the ends of the Earth," he pledged solemnly, his hand over his heart for good measure, and Olivia let out an exaggerated sigh.

"So gallant," she teased. "I'm so glad you're here."

She unlocked her car with her key fob and tried to nudge Noah out of the way, but he refused to move. Instead, he reached over to lift the door handle and then opened the door for her so she could slip behind the wheel. "So, where are we going?" he asked.

"Shopping," she replied with a smile. "And I need someone to hold my purse."

TWENTY MINUTES LATER, Noah found himself in a too-small chair outside a single-stall dressing room in a store called Back on the Rack. It was an eclectic, consignment-type shop where Olivia apparently spent a lot of time, judging by the way she seemed to be on a first-name basis with the employees.

"What do we think of this one?" she asked suddenly, and Noah heard the lock slide clear on the changing room door. Olivia opened it and stepped out wearing an oversized sweatshirt that looked like it was made from the fur of an oddly colored animal.

"I think somebody killed Elmo," he deadpanned, and Olivia gave him a look, one hand on her hip.

"That's not helpful," she replied.

"It *is* helpful!" Noah insisted, putting her purse on the ground and rising to his feet. "Now all you have to do is decide whether or not you *want* to wear the carcass of a beloved children's character. If the answer is no, we put it back."

Olivia's expression shifted, and it looked like she was trying not to laugh.

Noah decided to push a little harder. "Hello, children!" he said in cartoonish falsetto. "Elmo loves you! Elmo will keep you warm!"

"Oh, shut up," Olivia said, her voice wavering as she tried not to react, and she turned to go change again, but Noah looped his arms around her waist from behind.

"No! Don't go! Elmo wants to be your friend!" he continued, still using his character voice.

Olivia finally gave in, and her laughter filled the small space. Noah reveled in the sound; he loved making her laugh now just as much as he had the first time . . . and maybe more. She squirmed, trying to free herself from his hold, and he was suddenly very aware of the way she fit inside his arms. She was just the right height, not too wide or too thin, and he didn't feel like he was going to break her with the slightest pressure. He *did,* however, feel an almost uncontrollable urge to tuck his face against her neck and press his mouth to the tender skin there—just to see what she'd do.

He could. He *was* supposed to be her "boyfriend" after all. And if he did, it would undoubtedly push her past her limits. He was moments away from putting this whole charade to rest!

But they'd been having fun—her trying on outfits and him offering his unhelpful opinions. Did he really want to ruin it all by crossing those invisible lines right here, right now?

He loosened his arms and backed away.

"I'm gonna see if I can find you Oscar the Grouch," he said. "He's got to be in here somewhere."

Olivia laughed again as she went to change. "See if he comes in knee-length!" she called after she'd shut the flimsy door behind herself. "Green is a good color for me."

Yes, it is, Noah thought as he picked up her purse. He didn't want anyone to steal it, after all; he was only doing his duty.

He wandered out onto the sales floor and flipped almost absentmindedly through racks of women's shirts, skirts and dresses. Then he spent an abnormal amount of time peering at something called a romper that seemed to be a top and a bottom sewn together into one piece. He picked one up at random and carried it back to the dressing room.

"Hey, Pix?" he asked, raising his voice so she could hear him. "How do you pee in this?"

"How do I . . . what?" she asked. There was a muffled knocking noise and then the door opened, revealing her wearing a pair of black jeans and a dark-orange blouse with an opening along her collarbone.

Noah held the romper a bit higher. "How do you pee in this?" he asked again, genuinely curious, and Olivia burst into laughter.

"Umm . . . you have to take the whole thing off," she explained, her face bright with amusement.

Noah looked down at the garment again. "The whole thing? Like, every time?"

"Yeah, but it's not a big deal," she said with a shrug.

Noah tried and failed to wrap his mind around why a girl would want to go through so much trouble just to use the bathroom. He ultimately decided to file the information under "things I don't understand about women."

Olivia reached out and rubbed the romper's material between her fingers. "This is cute, actually. Did they have any mediums?" she asked.

Noah honestly didn't know.

"Would you go look for me, honey bug?" she asked sweetly, batting her eyes. She ran her hand down his arm, and he found himself following the motion with his eyes, even when he hadn't meant to. Something about her felt especially magnetic today, more so than usual. He'd always been drawn to her in a scientific sort of way—like he was conducting an experiment and wanted to record the results—but this was . . . different.

Biology, remember? his mind chided. *Oxytocin, dopamine, serotonin. There's a logical reason for this. Don't overanalyze it.*

He drifted obediently back toward where he'd found the romper, distantly wondering why being sent to find another size didn't bother him. It *should* bother him. This whole thing *should* bother him! He had other things to do tonight; he had a test in two days that he should be studying for and every piece of clothing he owned needed to be washed. So w*hy* was he so chill about being an errand boy instead?

I owe her for the ride, he rationalized. Besides that, he was still playing a role, just like she obviously was. Would she be making him carry her stuff and fetch her more clothes if she weren't trying to get under his skin? Probably not. It was all part of the game.

A game you had a chance to end, and didn't, a small voice reminded him.

Shut up, he told himself, and he jammed the unwanted garment back onto the rack. He flipped through the outfits nearby until he found one in a medium, and then he brought it back to the dressing room and hung it over the top of the door. "Special delivery! I want to see this one next," he declared. Olivia said something that sounded like an agreement, and Noah went back to his chair to wait.

"Wow, you did good, Campbell," she said in audible surprise a few minutes later. "Alright, are you ready?"

Noah leaned against the back of the chair and laced his fingers behind his head. "Yes," he answered, and the door opened.

What he'd thought was another romper was, in fact, a dress—a mossy, green dress with a brown belt around the waist. The hemline was cut higher in the front than the back, and the loose sleeves came almost to her elbows. She looked like some kind of garden fairy—one who could make flowers bloom with a touch of her hand.

Like a pixie.

Olivia pursed her lips, though she seemed pleased by his silence. "I don't think you were ready," she said softly.

No, I don't think I was, he thought. He'd seen her dressed up before, of course, but this was different somehow. This was a softer, less intentional sort of pretty—the kind that actually came from the inside and not from layers of makeup and lace.

He didn't know how many moments passed before Olivia

broke the stillness with a clearing of her throat. "I think I'll wear it to Mom's party this weekend. It's her fiftieth, so we're doing semiformal. No jeans allowed," she said. It almost sounded like she was talking just to fill the silence. "Do you still want to come?"

That got Noah's attention at last. "Come? To what?" he asked.

Olivia cocked her head. "To my mom's birthday party. It's Saturday, in Clarksville." She paused to casually examine her nails, though Noah got the feeling it wasn't casual at all. "Most of my family will be there, so I don't blame you if you'd rather skip it. Cohen men can be pretty intimidating."

She met his eye, and there was a clear challenge on her face. *Back out, Campbell*, she seemed to say. *I dare you.*

"Sure, I'd love to," he heard himself answer.

Wait . . . what?!

He had a moment of panic, a fleeting second where he wondered what had possessed him to say such a thing, but then, it faded, and he realized he was actually curious to see what kind of people had created the woman standing in front of him. He'd never met a date's parents before. Girls in high school hadn't taken him home because they knew he lived in the projects and, while he was great for a good time now and then, he wasn't the kind of catch you brought home to daddy. In college, he'd simply never gotten that far with anyone. There was a piece of him—a small piece—that wanted to prove he could do it, that he was worthy.

And if not for her, then who?

"You . . . you'd love to?" she repeated, almost like she couldn't believe her ears.

"Yeah. It sounds like fun," Noah confirmed, and a flicker of something odd crossed Olivia's face. She'd clearly expected him to draw the line at meeting her parents, but he hadn't, and now she was scrambling.

Well, you did *say you were going all-in,* that small voice reminded him, and he let himself smile as Olivia spun away.

There was no turning back now.

⁂

OLIVIA LEANED ACROSS the pockmarked wooden table and snagged one of Noah's french fries from the red plastic basket in front of him. It was the fourth or fifth one she'd stolen after making a big deal of not wanting any for herself, and she was waiting for his complacency to break.

Because it *had* to break, right?

He'd watched her purse and waited patiently while she'd wasted his time in the changing room. He hadn't batted an eye when she'd asked him to bring her outfits in new sizes or colors. He'd even agreed to meet her family this weekend!

Yeah, what are you going to do about that? a voice asked, and Olivia had to admit she was drawing a blank. This whole time she'd always figured that if she couldn't shake Noah before her mom's birthday party, then inviting him home would be the line in the sand. Surely he wouldn't cross it just to spend the weekend playacting in front of a bunch of people he'd never met?

Surely *she* wouldn't let him?

You didn't have to ask, you know, the voice reminded her. *If you didn't want to take him, you could have just let him forget.*

Olivia silently rebuked herself. That ship had sailed now, and she was going to have to ride it.

Somehow.

Noah reached up to scratch the back of his neck, and Olivia saw a sepia-toned tattoo peek from beneath the edge of his sleeve. She'd noticed it a few times before but hadn't felt comfortable asking about it. But now . . . now she wanted to know. She reached across the table and took hold of his wrist before pulling his arm closer to her.

"What is this?" she asked. She pushed the fabric higher before tracing her fingertip over the twists and turns of the complicated design inked into his skin. A rash of goose bumps rushed across his wrist and up toward his elbow, but he didn't pull away.

"It's a birthmark," he said.

She stared at him skeptically, one eyebrow raised. "A birth-mark?" she repeated. "That looks like a sailor's knot?"

"Yes. I come from a long line of seafaring men."

"And you were born with it?"

"How else does one get a birthmark?"

She pursed her lips, and he smirked at her—obviously aware of the frustration he was causing. "No, really," she insisted.

She saw him glance from side to side and then twist to look behind their booth. When he turned back to her, he leaned across the tabletop and beckoned for her to do the same. "Alright, I'll tell you, but you have to keep it a secret," he said when they met in the middle.

Olivia's curiosity spiked to dangerous levels, but she eyed him with suspicion. "Okay . . ."

He looked to either side again, then looked down and pointed to where her fingers still rested on his arm. "It's a brand. I got it when I joined the mafia."

Olivia jolted away and released his arm, shaking her head at her own gullibility. "Noah Campbell!" she exclaimed. "You are full of it."

He laughed and settled back in his seat. Then he crossed his arms over his chest and stretched his legs out beneath the table—which Olivia knew because one of them was suddenly pressed against hers from the knee down.

But she didn't move it.

That would show weakness, she told herself, although something in the back of her mind knew that wasn't the reason.

"Why won't you just tell me?" she asked again.

Noah smirked from his seat. "Because it requires a blood sacrifice, and I'm too pretty to die," he said.

Olivia snorted. "That's a matter of opinion," she replied.

He retrieved another french fry from his basket and then pushed the remaining pile toward her. So, he *had* noticed her thievery. Interesting.

"Do you have any?" he asked, and Olivia had to remember he wasn't talking about fries.

"What, birthmarks?" she shot back.

"Or tattoos, whichever."

She crunched on a handful of his cast-off treats. Now that he'd given them freely, there was no reason to sneak them one by one. "No," she admitted. "I've thought about getting three birds somewhere for me and Michael and Danny—"

"Who?"

"My brothers."

"Oh yeah, the Marines."

She nodded, surprised that he'd remembered that tidbit of information. "Yeah, but I can never decide for sure where to put them, so I haven't had it done. Someday, maybe."

There was a lull in the conversation, and Noah nudged her leg with his. "So, you said your family is scary, but like, *how* scary?"

Olivia smiled and took a drink from her straw. "Are you having second thoughts?"

"No, I just want to be prepared. I mean, do I need to increase my insurance plan or something?"

She laughed. "No, but my dad will probably threaten you with bodily harm."

"Can't be any worse than his daughter."

"When have I ever threatened you?" she demanded, and Noah scoffed loudly before leaning his elbows on the table.

"Umm, let's see, I believe you once threatened to scoop out my eyeballs with a spoon," he started, ticking items off on his fingers. "Then you said your brothers could remove my arms and beat me with them, and *then* there's the unforgettable time you mentioned castration."

Olivia laughed and mirrored his position. "Alright, the first one is legit, but the arms thing is something *Danny and Michael* would do, not me personally, and the castration comment was meant for Lexie's old boyfriend, Colt."

"Even so, you were very committed to the concept, which was frightening."

She chuckled again and wondered how exactly she'd ended up having dinner with Noah and actually *having fun* when she'd intended to go straight home from work and curl up under a blanket with a bowl of popcorn. "What's your family like? Any siblings?" she asked. For some reason, she pictured a whole horde of little pranksters with dark hair and mischievous eyes.

Noah's expression shifted slightly, becoming more guarded than it had been, and he seemed to focus on something over her shoulder. "Nope, just me," he said lightly.

"And what about your parents? Who taught you to cook?"

"My mom," he answered. "She's a chef." He pulled away from her and lifted his drink before draining the rest of the glass in one long swallow.

"Oh! No wonder, then," Olivia said in surprise. "What does your dad do?"

Noah brought the glass down to the tabletop with a thunk that rattled the basket of fries. "He's a magician," he said curtly, his eyes hard. "Are you wanting to leave Friday or Saturday?"

Olivia furrowed her brow at his unexpected reaction and the abrupt change of subject. Had he really said his dad was a *magician*? Was that a real answer or—

"And what should I bring to wear? You said no jeans."

Olivia didn't respond right away. Instead, she scanned his face for further explanation, but it was like he'd wiped it blank. Apparently, she'd found a touchy subject. "Saturday morning," she said, "coming back Sunday afternoon, if that's okay? And maybe dress pants for the party."

Noah nodded in acknowledgement and let out a quiet breath that Olivia only noticed because his shoulders visibly relaxed, like maybe he'd been afraid she would push for more information. "Sunday is fine," he said. Then his normal impish smirk returned to his face. "Do I get to bunk with you?"

Olivia narrowed her eyes and leveled him with a serious stare. "You'll sleep on the couch in the den, and the stairs will be booby trapped," she told him.

Noah stuck out his lower lip in a childish pout that almost made her laugh. "We don't even get to share a bathroom?" he whined.

She shook her head firmly. "If you talk like that, we won't even share a roof. My dad is not above pitching you a tent in the driveway."

He grimaced. "So, you're telling me to be on my best behavior?"

"Yes."

"I don't know if that's possible."

"I'm sure you can find a way."

He groaned as if this would be a huge imposition, and Olivia did her best not to worry. She didn't know how the weekend would go, but she did know one thing for sure: it would be nothing if not interesting.

14

NOAH WAS STANDING in the kitchen on Saturday morning, munching the last few spoonfuls of a bowl of cereal and vaguely hoping he'd remembered to put clean underwear in his duffel bag, when a car horn sounded from outside. He sighed and poured his leftover milk down the drain before rinsing his bowl and setting it on the leaning tower of dishware in the sink. Normally he would wash his own dishes, but Conner had so many to do already that one more wouldn't make any difference.

He flung the strap of his bag over one shoulder and headed to the garage with a distinct feeling of unease in his chest. Keeping up the charade with Olivia was one thing, but he didn't want to lie to her family. He wasn't a liar—he *hated* liars—but every step he took closer to her car felt like one more move in that direction. He crossed the washed-out gravel driveway toward the idling Mustang before yanking open the passenger's side door.

"Good morning, honey bug!" Olivia said cheerfully.

"Morning," he mumbled back. He tossed his duffel into the back seat before sliding in beside her. "Hey, do you mind if I study while you drive?" he asked. He hoped focusing his attention on something besides their destination would help settle his nerves.

She shrugged and took a sip from the silver thermos in her hand. "No. Are you worried about an exam?"

"A little," he admitted, twisting in his seat so he could unzip the top of his bag and retrieve a thick textbook from the inside. He settled the book on his lap and buckled his seat belt, both literally and figuratively.

"It's okay if you're too busy to come. You can stay home and study if you need to," she offered, and Noah met her gaze head-on.

"Do you want me to come?" he asked bluntly. He didn't want to intrude if she truly didn't want him there; this was her chance to give both of them an out.

Olivia's smile froze for a second, and then she covered it with the thermos again and took another sip. "Mom is excited to meet you," she said once she'd swallowed.

That didn't answer his question, but Noah chose not to press the issue. He was packed; he was in the car; he was going. End of discussion. "Alright, then it's settled," he told her, and he offered what he hoped was a reassuring smile.

Olivia studied him for another second before replacing her thermos in the center cupholder and putting the Mustang into reverse. "Okay, away we go!" she declared as the car backed out onto the asphalt. Seconds later they were flying down State Route 22, and Noah was trying to focus on the chapter headings in the book in front of him.

But it only took ten minutes for him to decide it wasn't going to work. This had to be the most boring class he'd ever taken, and the words were simply bouncing around inside his skull like ping-pong balls. It didn't help that the whole car smelled like her, and the sharp, citrus scent was making his brain fuzzy. He looked over at Olivia, who had remained surprisingly quiet while he was reading, and caught her peeking toward the pages in his lap.

"What is all of that?" she asked when she met his eye.

He sighed and settled deeper into the seat cushions. *"Evaluation and Assessment of Psychomotor Skills,"* he parroted, reading straight from the cover of the book. "It's riveting."

"Sounds like it," she said dryly, and she lifted her drink with the hand that wasn't on the wheel. "So, a physical therapist, huh?"

"Yep."

"Why?"

"Well, all the underwater basket-weaving classes were full."

"Too bad, since that's such a lucrative field and all," she teased. She put her thermos down and glanced at him again. "But seriously, why?"

"So I can make grown men cry."

"That's not a reason!"

"It is, too!" he insisted. "We're not all out to save the world, you know."

She smiled and shook her head. Then she looked over as he set the book on the floor behind her seat. "Well, if you're not doing that, do you want to play a game?"

"Like what?"

She slowed and made a left turn at a flashing yellow light. "In high school, we used to play 'Liar, Liar' on long trips. Do you know that one?"

Noah shook his head, forgetting she couldn't hear the gesture. "No, but it sounds self-explanatory," he answered.

"Pretty much. You tell me something, and I have to decide

if I think you're telling the truth or not. If I guess right, I get a point, but if you fool me, you get the point."

"Gotcha," he said with a nod. "Your game, so you go first."

Olivia chewed on her lower lip as she followed the highway to the right and made her way around the county courthouse. "Alright, I've got one," she said. "Believe it or not, I took ballet as a kid."

She glanced his way, and Noah narrowed his eyes as he tried to picture a younger Olivia in a tutu and tights. Try as he might, he just couldn't do it. "False," he said firmly, and Olivia grinned.

"True!" she shouted. "But I only lasted four weeks."

"What, did you flunk out?"

"Nope. I was asked to leave."

"You were asked to leave a *kid's ballet class*?"

"Yep," she said, the word popping from her mouth. "Apparently I kept putting the other girls in headlocks."

Noah felt his face light up in delight. Now *that* was an image he could understand.

Olivia saw his expression and shrugged in a self-deprecating sort of way. "I don't fight without a reason, so they probably deserved it."

"Aww, my little psycho!" Noah teased, and she reached over to smack his chest with the back of her hand.

For whatever reason, he didn't mind.

"Your turn," she reminded him.

He sighed; at least with this kind of game he got to choose what information he gave away. After a few moments, he shifted in his seat. "I once sold sunscreen to a naked man," he offered.

Olivia whipped her head in his direction before quickly turning back to the road. "You *what*?!" she exclaimed. "Okay, you definitely made that up. Unless you were at a roadside stand or something, but even then."

"A roadside stand that sells sunscreen?"

"You know what I mean! Something other than a regular store."

"Nope, right there at Watson's Grocery, lane two," Noah confirmed, and he watched her eyes grow even wider. "He showed up in his birthday suit, and one of the managers—I'll let you guess which one—told him he could come in if he covered himself. So, the guy finds an old sweatshirt from someplace, ties it backwards around his waist '90s-style, and waltzes right in."

"No! But that wouldn't even—"

"Cover everything? Yeah, I'm aware."

She gaped in disbelief, and Noah felt a surge of satisfaction at having provided a tidbit she found so entertaining. Of course, everyone found that story entertaining; how could you not?

"So, all of that is true?" she asked.

"Cross my heart," he assured her.

"Wow . . . I have no words, just . . . wow." She adjusted the thermostat and turned the radio down a little, like that would help her think. "Okay, so my dad was in the military for most of my life, and I've lived in six states and three foreign countries."

He studied her, searching for signs of deceit, but saw nothing obvious. "I'm going to say . . . true?" he guessed.

She grinned again, and her smile felt like the sun coming out from behind the clouds. Noah did an internal double take. Since when had he started creating poetic similes for the way she looked at him? He obviously hadn't gotten enough sleep.

"Only four states, not six," she admitted, "so I win."

"Now, wait a minute!" Noah protested. He twisted in his seat to see her better. "That seems like a technicality!"

"True is true, and false is false," Olivia sang. She was far too happy about having slipped another point past him.

"Fine," he grumbled, "but this game is rigged."

An hour went by, then part of another, and the open fields of winter wheat gradually gave way to sprawling subdivisions, then blocks of towering apartment buildings, and then the urban sprawl of Clarksville proper. At some point in the drive, they'd transitioned from their game to simply telling stories, and Noah now knew about the time Olivia had accidentally stapled a cartoon drawing of her professor inside a research paper and the day she'd threatened Lexie's ex-boyfriend with a baseball bat.

"Worst kiss," she declared, deciding the next topic.

Noah groaned. "One time I got the wrong girl."

Olivia twisted toward him while she waited for a traffic light to change. "The wrong girl? Okay, that doesn't just *happen*," she insisted. "What's the story there?"

Noah scrubbed his palm across his mouth. "Well, this was in high school, and I'd been out with this girl, Anna, a few times," he explained. "On those dates, she'd neglected to mention—and I somehow hadn't found out—that she was an identical twin."

Olivia grimaced.

"So, one day after school, I saw her across the parking lot, and I thought, 'you know what? You've had fun, she likes you, why not walk over there and go for it?'"

Olivia winced again as the light turned green, but Noah went on.

"So, in my infinite teenage wisdom, I did. I walked right up to her, pulled her in and kissed her."

There was a heavy sort of pause, during which Olivia looked his way. "And . . . ?" she prompted.

"And," he said dramatically, "she punched me in the face."

Olivia laughed out loud and made a right turn. "It was the sister, wasn't it?"

"It *was* the sister," Noah confirmed. "The sister I didn't know existed until *after* I could open my eye again and thought I was seeing double."

"Did Anna at least know it was an accident? I mean, surely people had gotten them mixed up before," Olivia asked.

"Oh, no, she absolutely thought I'd done it on purpose," Noah grumbled, remembering the aftermath.

"No benefit of the doubt?"

"Nope—just threw me straight into the high school rumor mill. Before the week was out, the story had gone from a simple mix-up to a brawl with school security after I tried to force a girl into my car."

Olivia's expression immediately shifted from humor to disbelief. "You're *kidding*!" she replied. "People really said you did that?"

Noah shrugged and looked out the passenger's side window. This wasn't a part of high school he revisited all that often. "Why not? I was new that year, I lived on the wrong side of town, and I was, apparently, capable of anything." He tried to keep his voice light, but even he could hear the bitterness that lingered in it.

Another quiet moment passed, during which Olivia turned off the highway and onto a narrower road. Then she reached over and wrapped her fingers around his hand where it rested on the leg of his jeans. Noah glanced down at where her skin touched his and was surprised that his hand itself wasn't glowing orange.

It sure felt like he was on fire.

He cleared his throat and kept talking, mostly because he didn't want to fixate on the unexpected sensation. "It worked out in the end, though; life's a lot easier when you learn to let people assume whatever they want. Expectations are lower that way," he said. "If you ask anyone I graduated with, they'd probably tell you I was a hardened criminal with a line of broken hearts a mile long."

Olivia's thumb brushed over the back of his hand, and Noah felt lightning travel up his arm and lodge somewhere beneath his collarbone.

"But you weren't," she said, and he was amazed by the way it didn't sound like a question.

He huffed out a breath and pushed his free hand through his hair. "Reports were greatly exaggerated," he admitted.

Olivia smiled faintly before taking her hand back and using it to turn left into a subdivision. "And what about in college? Is the line a mile long now?"

Noah considered her question carefully before answering, thinking back to all the girls he'd flirted with and all the nights that hadn't meant very much. Then he flattened his hair where he'd made it stand on end. "Reports are greatly exaggerated," he repeated.

Her expression grew thoughtful, and Noah passed his eyes across her face before looking out the window again. Two-story, brick houses rose on either side of the road, separated from each other by tall, wooden privacy fences. This was the kind of neighborhood he'd lived in before his father had left—before the day everything had fallen apart. It was the kind of neighborhood he'd only been welcome back in as the hired help.

Olivia turned into an immaculate driveway where three other cars were already parked alongside the house. Then she cut off the engine, though she kept both hands tight on the wheel. "Okay, this is home. You ready?"

Noah watched uncertainty skip across her face and wondered—again—what she'd told her parents about him. "Are *you*?" he asked.

She let out a long breath and reached for her door handle. "We'll see," she said, though the words were nearly lost as she opened her door and the jarring sound of a nail gun filled the car's interior. Somebody was hard at work somewhere.

"Livvy!" came a voice from the porch.

Noah looked through the windshield and saw a woman coming through the front door—a woman with olive skin and dark hair that fell in a braid down her back. She had a baby propped on her hip, and there was no possible way she was Olivia's mother.

"Issa!" Olivia shouted as she climbed from the car.

Noah did the same and stood awkwardly while the women greeted each other.

"Noah, this is my sister-in-law, Issa, and my niece, Aria," Olivia said. She cooed the last words in the direction of the child, who closed her tiny fists around her mother's shirt and held on.

"Noah?" Issa asked, not bothering to lower her voice. Her gaze slid down to Noah's feet in unabashed curiosity. "I thought you said you were bringing a friend."

"He *is* a friend," Olivia hissed, and Issa's eyes seemed to light up even more.

"Well, hello then, Friend Noah! Welcome to Casa di Cohen," she said. Her voice was soft and lilting and carried a hint of somewhere far away. Definitely European.

Noah stepped forward quickly and shook the hand she offered. "Glad to meet you. Issa, is it?"

"Yes, short for Isabella. I'm Michael's wife," Issa explained. "Come on, I'll show you where everyone is." Then, she turned and went back through the front door, still talking to Olivia as she went. "Your mom is having a spa day with Aunt Tammy, and the guys are still assembling the gazebo. They've only got five hours until we need to decorate, so I hope they make it."

Noah followed quietly behind, his head on swivel as they made their way through a spacious living area with an open kitchen. The interior of the house was fairly quiet, but the sound of men arguing entered the moment Issa opened the back door.

"That side should face out."

"No, it matches the others."

"Then they should *all* face out!"

"Hey, guys!" Issa called, but to no avail.

"Shouldn't we have seven railings? There are only six in this pile."

"Hey, guys!" Issa shouted again, this time rising above the noise. "Livvy and her boyfriend are here."

Suddenly, there was silence.

The men—obviously Olivia's father and brothers—froze where they stood, and all three heads whipped toward the porch as if by synchronized command.

Olivia glared at her sister-in-law, who only smiled.

"Have fun!" Issa sang as she elbowed Olivia in the ribs and turned to go inside. As she passed Noah, she paused and leaned closer so only he could hear. "They're not as scary as they act. Be brave," she advised, and then she was gone.

The click of the door shutting behind her was the only sound that registered in Noah's mind as the Cohen men continued to stare at him like he had a bullseye on his forehead. He swallowed and reminded himself not to slouch.

"Hey, baby girl," Mr. Cohen drawled as he approached the porch. He pulled Olivia into a hug that probably could have snapped her in half, if he'd wanted it to. "Now, who have you brought with you?" he asked, acknowledging Noah at last.

"Daddy, this is Noah Campbell," Olivia started. "Noah, this is my dad, Roger Cohen."

"Nice to meet you, sir," Noah said, holding his hand out first. The older man took it with a nod of his head.

"I didn't know you were bringing more muscle," Mr. Cohen told his daughter. "Although another set of hands won't hurt, I guess." He looked Noah up and down, but in a very different way than Issa had. "You ready to be useful, young man?"

"Yes, sir," Noah replied. He hadn't realized this trip would include manual labor, but there was no way he could answer otherwise. Besides, it would be nice to have something to do with his hands.

"Good," Mr. Cohen responded. "Then let's put you to work."

Four hours later, Noah was sweating like a pig and wondering what the penalty would be for taking off his sweatshirt. The others already had, though he didn't think the option extended to him—especially not since Olivia was still in the yard. He looked up from where he was spreading creek gravel around a newly installed fire pit, his eyes automatically seeking her out. He found her partway up a ladder, where she was wrapping a long strand of fairy lights around the trunk and limbs of a thick oak tree. Issa stood with one foot on the bottom rung while her daughter played in the grass nearby.

"You're staring awfully hard, Campbell," Danny Cohen said from where he was stringing the same type of lights through the now-finished gazebo.

"What?" Noah asked, yanking his attention back to his work.

"I said you're staring awfully hard," Danny repeated, a little slower this time. "That's my baby sister over there, and she's not interested in boys . . . or kissing or"—he wrinkled his nose—"anything else, so pay attention to what you're doing."

Noah exhaled and went back to smoothing the gravel evenly from the fire pit to the outer ring of landscaping rock.

"Lay off him, Dan. Liv deserves to be happy," said another voice, and Michael—the older brother—came out of the garage nearby. He set a stack of Adirondack chairs beside the gazebo and straightened up. "That said, though, if you hurt her, we will find you," he told Noah, his index finger pointed menacingly.

Noah nodded in acknowledgement as the two men began discussing which form of torture would be most appropriate for someone who broke their sister's heart—the options ranging from arctic exposure to unsedated exploratory surgery. Noah finished with the gravel and arranged the lawn chairs in a comfortable circle around the new fire pit, refusing to let the argument unnerve him. He could stare at Olivia until he drilled holes in the back of her head, and her brothers still wouldn't have anything to worry about. She'd always been very clear about what she wanted—and *didn't* want—and he . . . well, he fell into the latter category.

Danny and Michael went inside to shower just as Olivia finished hanging her lights. She waved to Noah before scooping Aria up from the ground. Then she started to cross the yard in his direction, but Mr. Cohen cut her off.

"Go on in, Livvy, and start cleaning up," he directed. "Me and Junior need to have a chat."

Noah tensed, his hands on the back of one of the lawn chairs, and he watched as Olivia laid a hand on her father's arm.

"Daddy," she warned, her voice low, but Mr. Cohen shook his head.

"He's a grown man, Livvy. He can handle himself," he admonished.

Noah caught Olivia's eye for a second, and she looked like she still wanted to object, but she bit her tongue.

"Alright, but he needs to be in one piece for dinner," she said, and then she crossed the back porch and went into the house.

Noah straightened and shoved his hands into the pockets of his dirty blue jeans; there was no point in acting like he hadn't been listening.

Mr. Cohen's worn-out work boots crunched against the creek gravel Noah had laid around the fire pit, and he chose one of the blue chairs to Noah's right. "Sit down, son," he ordered, gesturing to the next seat. "I've got a few things to say."

15

LATER, NOAH TOWEL-DRIED his hair and did his best to make it behave. Then he dressed in khaki pants and a green button-up shirt he'd borrowed from Jake. When he felt presentable, he opened the bathroom door and stepped out into the upstairs hall. All the other doors had been closed when he'd gone to shower, but now the closest two were open, revealing rooms with impeccably made queen-size beds and suitcases on the floor. One had a portable baby bed in the far corner, which meant it belonged to Michael and his family, leaving the second to Danny by default.

Which must mean . . .

Noah crept along the hall to the farthest bedroom, unsure exactly what he hoped to find, and discovered that the door was cracked. Someone was definitely moving around inside. He knocked hesitantly on the doorframe. "Hey, Pix? It's me," he called.

"Come in!" she answered, and he pushed the door open with one hand, peeking around the edge as he did. He didn't know what he'd expected . . . Red and black, maybe? Rock-and-roll posters? It certainly wasn't the soft, feminine colors she had everywhere.

The walls were powder blue, and there were gauzy green curtains over a window that faced the backyard. Her bed was covered in a fluffy white comforter with what looked like colorful wildflowers embroidered on the bottom half, and a canvas painting of mountains hung above the wooden headboard.

Olivia was sitting in a chair in front of a vanity mirror, already wearing the green dress he'd accidentally picked out. "So, you survived," she commented, sparing his reflection a glance as she wrapped a section of her hair around a curling iron.

Noah shrugged and leaned one shoulder against the doorframe, his arms crossed over his chest. "It wasn't that bad, actually; he didn't even show me his gun collection. I've been led to believe that was pretty standard when meeting a girl's dad."

Olivia half laughed. "That's surprising, actually. There's basically a bunker in the basement." She unwound a long ringlet from the wand and turned her head from side to side, examining her handiwork. Then she picked up a curl from near the edge of her face and pulled it around to the back of her head before securing it with a bobby pin from the dresser top.

Noah watched as one pin joined another, and whatever Olivia was creating began to take shape. His mind drifted back to the conversation in the yard.

"You're a curiosity, son," Mr. Cohen said. "You're the first friend from school Livvy's ever brought home who didn't have both X chromosomes. You must have done something right to get this far, and I'd be doing you a disservice if I wasn't up front with you from the beginning.

"That girl in there deserves the best, and not just because she's my little girl, but because she's a good person. She's sassy, sure, and probably too stubborn for her own good, but she's also fiercely loyal

to those she cares about. She has the biggest, deepest, purest heart of anyone I've ever known, and whoever she chooses to give it to will be one of the luckiest men alive.

"But don't be mistaken—she doesn't need you. She doesn't need anyone; her mother and I raised her that way on purpose. So, if she ever does choose you, it's because she wants *you—and that's an honor you cannot imagine. It's an honor that should be respected and protected with your life. Do you understand?"*

"Yes, sir, I do."

"Do you feel you deserve an honor like that?"

"No, sir, I don't."

Mr. Cohen studied him hard, his mouth in a firm line that never wavered. "Good, because you don't now, and you won't fifty years from now, either. But that's how we know we're the lucky ones."

"There," Olivia proclaimed, breaking Noah from his reverie. She rose to stand. "What do you think?"

He blinked a few times and realized that while he'd been distracted, she'd swapped from regular pins to clips with tiny white flowers on them. They were tucked here and there among the loose curls that made a crown-like loop around the back of her head. He cleared his throat, suddenly aware that he hadn't actually said anything the whole time he'd been preoccupied. Normally, he would have been uncomfortable with such a silence, but this time he hadn't even noticed it.

"You look great!" he said. Then he pushed off the doorframe and ventured a few steps into the room. "One thing, though?" he added, stopping when they were toe-to-toe. He raised one hand and hesitated, waiting for a green light, and when she nodded, he gently freed one small curl near her face. He twirled it around his index finger before letting it lay softly against her temple. "I like it like this," he murmured, and without having planned it, the backs of his fingers drifted down across her cheek—almost like they'd chosen to do so of their own accord.

Her gaze held his, and something electric passed between them.

Noah's mouth went dry, and he automatically wet his lips. He could kiss her. Right there, in her room, he could do it again. Memories flashed through his mind like picture slides: Olivia's hair sliding through his fingers on New Year's Eve, the flush in her cheeks before she'd pulled him in for a second kiss, the way he'd been able to feel her in his blood.

But he hesitated a moment too long.

"Livvy!" Issa called from downstairs. "Hurry! Your mom's turning into the driveway!"

Olivia's eyes went wide, and she turned away all at once. "Come on!" she urged, hurrying into the hall. "I don't want to miss her face when she sees the yard!"

Noah followed slowly, turning a strange feeling over and over in his mind. It wasn't the disappointment of a moment missed; it was . . . something else. Something that felt too big to describe. Something that seemed . . . new.

༄

THE PARTY WAS a success! Olivia looked around the crowded yard with pride as her mother's friends and family served themselves from a catered buffet table and talked in animated groups. The playlist she'd created of all her mom's favorite songs played through Bluetooth speakers that were placed strategically around the yard, and several of their guests had found enough space on the grass to dance.

"This song reminds me of you," Noah said, and Olivia met his eye as he took an empty Chinet plate from her hands and dumped it into an outdoor garbage can. Her ears tuned in to a familiar set of chords, and she felt her brows rise.

"'Thunderstruck'?" she asked.

Noah chuckled and drained the last of his drink before throwing the cup away. "Yeah. It was playing in your car the day we met," he explained.

"How do you remember that?" she asked incredulously.

He raised one shoulder in a shrug. "I don't know. I guess it's hard to forget when a beautiful woman actually leaves you in her dust."

She laughed and tucked a wayward curl behind her ear—the one he'd pulled out earlier. "I didn't do that. Did I?"

"Yes, ma'am, you did!" he confirmed. "You put on your sunglasses like some kind of Hollywood starlet, said 'good luck with your snake problem' and then hit the gas like you were joining the Indy 500. Dust everywhere; my uniform was a whole different color, and I couldn't breathe for weeks!"

"Oh, that's an exaggeration!"

"Not much of one," he replied.

Olivia turned back toward the table where they'd been sitting with her family, but their empty seats had been claimed by someone else.

"Move your feet, lose your seat, I guess," Noah said. Then he held his hand out in front of her in a clear invitation. "Want to dance instead?"

Olivia glanced down at his hand and then around the yard. The rest of her family was tied up with company, and there were other couples dancing close to the new gazebo. They wouldn't be the only ones, and it wasn't as if she had anything better to do anyway. Why not have some fun?

"Sure," she answered. She took his hand and let him lead her toward the far side of the yard. The fairy lights she'd strung earlier stretched above their heads like a spider's web, and Noah found a vacant patch of grass beyond the edges of the crowd as "Hurt So Good" poured from a nearby speaker.

He raised her arm and spun her in a quick circle, and Olivia found herself laughing even before she came back to face him. Noah turned out to be a pretty good dancer, even if it mostly consisted of twirling her in and out until she was dizzy and breathless. John Mellencamp faded into Modern English, and by the third or fourth song, Olivia could feel her face trying to split open from the force of her smile.

"Stop! I need water," she begged at last, but when she stepped back, his hand traveled down her arm and caught her by the wrist, as if he weren't quite ready to let her leave. "I'll be right back!" she assured him, reclaiming her hand. Then she made her way toward the house and the beverage table, though she barely felt her feet touch the ground. Instead, her entire body seemed to be buzzing—every cell alive with energy—and the places where Noah had touched her, however briefly, still felt like handprints on her skin.

But the thing was, she didn't hate it.

Though she *did* sort of hate the way she didn't hate it.

The simple truth, if she was being honest with herself, was that like it or not, Noah had weaseled his way into her life, and he was growing on her.

Like a wart, maybe, but growing nonetheless.

She reached for an empty cup and held it under the tap of a fancy drink dispenser.

"So, how long have you been together?" someone asked from over her shoulder, and Olivia didn't have to look to know it was Michael.

"Not long," she answered, filling her cup and turning to her brother. A pang of guilt speared through her at the lie, but she tried to ignore it. Noah wouldn't be around forever, and when he was gone, the exact details of their charade wouldn't matter.

Another sharp sting hit somewhere in her chest.

"Really?" Michael asked, obviously surprised. "You just seem very comfortable with him. It doesn't *look* new. In fact, if I didn't know any better, I'd say he's half in love with you already."

Olivia almost spit her drink in his face in surprise. "He's *what*?! No. I don't think so."

Michael smiled and raised his own cup toward where Noah was now standing with Issa, letting her use his arm as a support while she stood on one foot to fix her shoe. He had Aria balanced in the other arm, and the baby was diligently trying to chew on the collar of his shirt.

"You don't think so?" her brother asked. "He could be literally anywhere else, but instead he's here, wearing church clothes and pretending he likes spinach puffs, for no reason at all?"

"Maybe he actually likes spinach puffs," Olivia supplied.

But Michael shook his head. "Nah. He may not know it yet, but it's there. I'd put money on it."

Olivia took another sip of her drink and watched as Noah bounced Aria in his arms, her young laughter piercing the air. Noah Campbell, *in love with her*? No. The very idea was ridiculous! Noah didn't *do* love. He didn't *do* relationships. He didn't *do* complicated.

And yet . . . wasn't that exactly what they were? Complicated?

"No," she repeated at last. "No, he's just having a good time. It's a good party," she reasoned.

"Yeah, it's a good party," Michael agreed, "for a fifty-year-old woman he's never met."

Olivia considered this as her brother gave one last knowing smirk. Then he crossed the yard to his little family and took his daughter from Noah before tossing her easily into the air. Noah's attention drifted from the little girl to where Olivia stood staring, and she raised her hand in a small wave, trying to ignore the stutter-step in her chest.

Would it be so bad? a small voice asked, and Olivia mentally dug in her heels. Michael simply didn't know what he was talking about. She and Noah may have become friends despite her best efforts, but that was as far as it went.

Actually falling for him was out of the question.

16

NOAH LAID THE Super Soaker against Olivia's windshield and tucked an index card beneath it. Then, he ducked behind the base of an oak tree several yards away and pressed his back against the bark. Voices drifted over from the social sciences building, and Noah tensed before peeking through a fork in the tree's trunk. He had a clear view of Olivia's Mustang, and he couldn't let her strike first. Not like last time.

He didn't have to wait long. Olivia came down the sidewalk chatting with a friend, and their goodbyes filtered through the leaves that hid him as the girls parted ways. Olivia's footsteps came closer to his hiding place, but then they stopped abruptly.

"What the . . ." she said softly.

Noah craned his neck and watched as she slid the note from beneath the water gun. She said nothing, but he knew what she was reading.

"Defend yourself. Good luck."

She raised her head and looked around suspiciously. "Noah?" she called.

He laughed silently to himself. That hadn't taken her long!

"Noah?" she shouted again. "Don't you dare shoot me!"

But he didn't listen. He rarely did. Instead, he raised the barrel of his gun and fired through the fork in the tree, purposely splattering her windshield with water. "What's wrong, Warrior Princess?" he taunted. "Afraid to get wet?"

Olivia jumped back as his second shot rained down across her sneakers, and Noah was delighted to see a flash of determination streak across her face. He knew she wouldn't let a challenge like that go unanswered. She snatched the water gun from her hood and then yanked her driver's side door open and crouched behind it like a shield. "You're gonna get it, Campbell!" she yelled. "This means war!"

He snickered again and fired a shot directly at the window of her door. It wouldn't get her wet, but it would distract her long enough for him to change position. The water doused the glass, and he made a run for the next tree to the right, silently thanking whoever had landscaped the campus quad with so many convenient hiding places.

Sure enough, Olivia came up shooting, her stream of water aimed directly at the tree where he had been moments before. Noah held in another laugh as he ran in a crouch and slipped past a Jeep four spaces down from her car. He crept along the bumpers of three other vehicles before peeking around the last one. Olivia's door was still standing open . . . but she wasn't there.

"Gotcha!" a voice shouted, and a blast of lukewarm water drenched the right side of Noah's face before pouring down the front of his shirt. He stood and fired blindly across her trunk in the direction the shot had come from.

"Too slow!" she taunted, and Noah wiped the water from his eyes with one hand.

"Where did you go?" he demanded, ducking down behind her car again, and musical laughter met his ears from somewhere near the hood.

"I can't tell you that, now can I?" she teased, and Noah threw himself flat on his stomach. Sure enough, there was a pair of familiar blue tennis shoes near her front tire, and he fired beneath the vehicle in a sneak attack.

He was rewarded with a shriek of surprise, and the shoes jumped.

"You think you're slick, don't you?" she demanded, her voice filled with laughter, and Noah watched her feet move away over the grass. He pushed to his feet and ran along the line of vehicles before cutting up toward the sidewalk, intending to come around behind his original position. But again, he rounded the side of the tree line and found it empty. He peeked first around one large trunk and then into the space between two others. Then he scanned the parking lot again. Nothing.

Just as he was turning to double back, he heard a twig snap close by.

Too close.

Noah turned around, and another spray of water came down from above and soaked the front of his jeans. He looked up and saw Olivia wedged between two branches of a tree, the lowest of which was still above his head.

How did she get up there so fast?

He raised his weapon and fired, hitting his mark dead in the middle, and a wet spot bloomed across the center of Olivia's gray T-shirt, turning the material black. He ducked her return fire before drenching her a second time.

"Okay, okay, I call a truce," she spluttered, but Noah laughed.

"Only because you've cornered yourself!" he said. "That was a bad decision." Another stream of water hurtled down from the branches, but he saw it coming and sidestepped it easily. "So was not going high enough," he added, and he reached up to close a hand around her ankle. Then, he shook it.

"Stop that!" she shouted, though her voice wasn't afraid. She tried to yank her foot back, but he held on tight. With the other hand, he fired his gun again and turned the leg of her jeans a dark blue. "Noah!" she shrieked. "That's not fair!"

"Neither is turning into a squirrel, but here we are," he replied with a grin. Then he shook her leg again, and her shoe came loose from the bark.

She caught hold of the branch above her but dropped her gun, which clattered to the ground at his feet. "Noah, you're going to make me fall!"

Some of the water from her clothes dripped onto his face as he looked up at her perch, and suddenly he realized he had *missed her*. It had been a week since they'd gotten back from her parents' house, and while they had texted back and forth since then, it wasn't the same as actually being close to her.

He wanted her down from this tree.

Now.

"Come on, little squirrel," he said, tugging on the foot he still held in his hand. "It's time to jump."

"No," came her stubborn answer.

He tugged a little harder, and she laughed and clung to the branch over her head. "Come on, I'll catch you," he insisted.

"Umm, I think not."

"Don't you trust me?"

"Jury is still out."

The thing that had started growing in Noah's chest last weekend got a little bit bigger. He liked that she was having fun with him—fun that wasn't tied to earning points in some stupid game of emotional chicken.

Maybe we could have this all the time, he thought. *Maybe we could be . . . more.*

The thought made his whole body tense.

What does that mean? he asked himself.

It means what you think it means, idiot.

Yeah, but I've never . . .

Times change.

But I don't know how to . . .

Figure it out.

But she doesn't want me!

Then change her mind.

The finality of that thought rocked Noah's whole world. Just change her mind. It sounded easy, but was it possible? He looked up into Olivia's eyes, still wild with adrenaline, and tried to imagine never seeing her again—tried to imagine leaving her behind one day.

And he couldn't do it.

"Jump, Liv," he heard himself say, and her gaze locked onto his, almost as if she could hear the shift he felt inside. "Trust me," he went on. "I'll catch you."

Olivia took what seemed like a long, slow breath, and then, almost without warning, she let go of the tree. Noah dropped his water gun as she plummeted toward the earth, and then he caught her in both arms, just as he'd said he would.

She snaked her arms around his neck and kicked her feet like a child. "Alright, now put me down."

He put her feet on the ground but didn't fully release her. "What are you doing on Monday after work?" he asked.

She scanned his face, clearly caught off guard by the change of subject. "I don't think anything," she said. "Why?"

"I have a surprise for you."

Her nose scrunched up, and a wrinkle formed in the middle of her forehead. "Is it more water guns?"

Noah laughed and tried to soak in the feel of her standing in his arms. "No, no water guns. You'll like it, I promise."

She chuckled. "Well, then, no, I'm not doing anything."

"Good. Now you have plans."

"Now I have plans," she repeated, and he could hear a note of confusion that made him think she was still trying to figure out his angle.

But there was no angle—not this time.

He just had to figure out how to prove it.

MONDAY AFTERNOON, OLIVIA grabbed a bag from under her desk and changed quickly in the staff bathroom, swapping her pencil skirt and blouse for a pair of flowing, wide-legged pants and a top that slouched off one shoulder. She left her hair down but fluffed it out with both hands before leaning toward the mirror to touch up the wing on her eyeliner. She kept reminding herself that she'd been out with Noah before—she'd *made out* with Noah before!—so this shouldn't feel any different. And yet, for some reason, it *did*.

When she was done, she headed for the parking lot and found him standing behind her car, leaning against the trunk the same way he had the day he'd asked for a ride. Except this time, he was wearing nice jeans and a black T-shirt instead of his work uniform.

"Hey, Pixie. You ready to go?" he asked.

Olivia walked past him and popped the locks on her car before laying her work clothes in the back seat, silently reminding herself not to look too eager. "Where are we going?" she asked.

"That's for me to know and you to find out," he answered cryptically.

She shut her car door and immediately felt his hand against her lower back as he steered her away from her vehicle and toward his. As she slid into his passenger's seat, he leaned down and brushed his mouth against her ear. "You look amazing, by the way," he said, and a tingling wave of goose bumps washed down the side of her neck.

Keep it together, Cohen! she warned herself.

Though she was starting to think that might be harder than it sounded.

⤸⤷

"DO I WANT to know why you're so good at this?" Olivia asked, her arms crossed as she leaned against the side of an arcade game called "Sink It." Noah carefully aimed another ping-pong ball before bouncing it into one of several cup-shaped targets. The lights on the backboard flared to life, and the words "FIFTY POINTS" scrolled across the marquee in all caps.

He chuckled. "Probably not," he admitted. "Here, you want another turn?"

"Why, so you can mock me again? No, thanks. I'll take my air hockey win and go."

"Aww, come on. You can't be *that* bad," he coaxed. "Well, alright, you can't be that bad *twice*."

"What about that game?" she asked instead, pointing toward a massive console along the back wall. The outside was plastered with silhouettes of hip-hop dancers and a collection of pixelated arrows in various colors.

Noah's face went blank. "No," he said firmly.

"No? Why 'no'?" Olivia demanded, already backing toward the game's platform. "You danced with me before."

"That was different."

"Different how?" she taunted.

"One, it wasn't scored, and two, I was making it up as I went."

But she kept walking, ignoring his feeble protests.

"How about *you* play, and *I'll* watch," he compromised, finally following her across the arcade. The weekday crowd was thin, so they almost had the place to themselves.

"Oh, that's disappointing. I never took you for a coward." Olivia clicked her tongue disapprovingly. "But if you're scared to lose to a girl . . ."

Noah clenched his jaw and pressed his mouth into a thin line, and Olivia could see how much he hated the gauntlet being thrown down. He wouldn't be able to resist the challenge, especially when beating her would mean pulling ahead in their overall score.

"Fine," he finally huffed. "But this is coercion."

She cackled happily and stuffed arcade tokens into the game slots. The two platforms in the front lit up, and Noah took his place on the one beside her before using his foot to press a blue arrow on the floor.

"Battle round!" the machine declared.

"One way or another, you're going to regret this," he warned, and Olivia bounced on the balls of her feet as music surged through the game's speakers. She hadn't played this game since high school, but surely it would be like riding a bike. Right?

Colored arrows rose toward the top of the screen, and she stepped on the corresponding buttons in time with the beat of some random song. It took a few seconds, but she finally found her rhythm.

"Perfect! Nice one! Keep going!" the machine encouraged.

When she felt confident enough, she glanced over to see how Noah was doing, and a laugh burst from her chest. He looked less like he was dancing and more like he was hopping across hot coals. Most of his arrows missed their mark and turned gray as they reached the top of his screen.

"What do you call *that*?" she shouted over the music.

"Mind your own business!" he called back, and then he reached out and shoved her sideways, straight off her platform.

"Hey!" Olivia cried. She scrambled back up and tried to find her place in the song, but her momentum was gone.

"Oh, did I mess you up?" Noah asked innocently. "Here, let me help." He grabbed her arm and tugged her first to one side, then toward the back. "Look, this is how you do it."

"Let me go!" she cried, laughing. "This is *not* how you do it!" She tried to aim her feet toward the correct buttons, but Noah's "assistance" always sent her the wrong way.

When the song finally ended, their scores were both pathetic.

"Oh, look at that, I beat you by forty points! I really thought you'd be better at this," Noah said, his grin wide and his face flushed. He was breathing hard from his exertion. "Maybe you shouldn't trash-talk so hard. It's embarrassing."

"Maybe you should keep your hands to yourself!" she shot back. "That didn't count. Not a fair game."

"Totally a fair game. If you fell off, that's your problem."

"I fell off because *you pushed me*!"

"Irrelevant details. Are you hungry?"

"No, I'm not hungry! I want to annihilate you!"

"Mmm, no. The offer has expired. It's time for dinner," he answered. Then he bent down and grabbed her legs before tossing her over his shoulder in a fireman's carry.

"Noah Campbell!" Olivia yelled, though it was hard to push the words out while she was laughing. "Noah, put me down and let me beat you!"

"See, there you go threatening me again. What have I said about that?" he asked, surprisingly nonchalant as he carried a thrashing woman toward the parking lot.

"Aggh!" she huffed in frustration. Then she ducked her head as he went through the front door and stepped out into the crisp March evening. "I hate you."

"I know."

The world seemed to tilt on its axis as he put her down, though everything stilled again when she found herself wedged between his body and the side of his car. He raised his hand and tucked her hair behind her ear, and Olivia was automatically reminded of the last time she'd been in this position.

In a secluded summer house . . .

With the lights down low . . .

And fireworks exploding somewhere nearby . . .

"Tell me you cheated," she demanded stubbornly.

Noah's fingers drifted down the back of her neck. "I cheated," he admitted, his voice soft.

Suddenly, Olivia felt reckless. "So, what's my prize?" she asked.

The corner of Noah's mouth tipped up. "You can have it after dinner," he said, his smile growing as Olivia's eyes narrowed. Then he reached past her and pulled the handle on her door. "Come on."

ALMOST AN HOUR later, Olivia crumpled the wrapper of a food truck burger and tossed it into the trash can near their picnic table.

"Where did you *put* all of that?" Noah asked from beside her, his eyes wide, and Olivia raised her eyebrows.

"Excuse me? What does that mean?" she countered.

"It means you don't exactly have a figure that says 'I can eat two burgers, a bag of popcorn and a funnel cake in one sitting.'"

"Oh, really? And what does my figure say?"

"Warning: too hot to handle."

Olivia snorted and rolled her eyes. "Wow," she drawled, "that was cheesy. You got any other lines in there?"

Noah finished his nachos and rose to stand, discarding his trash the same way she had. "No, but I have something else," he said, reaching into his back pocket. He withdrew a square of white paper that appeared to be blank—at least as far as Olivia could tell.

"What's that?" she asked.

"Your prize," Noah replied. He came back and slung one leg over the bench so he was straddling it beside her. "Turn around," he ordered.

Olivia crossed her arms in protest. "I don't remember giving you permission to boss me around quite so much," she said, but Noah only grinned.

"I prefer to ask for forgiveness instead of permission," he quipped. "Now, turn." He twirled his index finger in a circle, and Olivia finally turned her back to him.

"Close your eyes," he said.

"But—"

"Are you going to argue about every single thing?"

Olivia almost laughed, though she bit down on her lip hard enough to keep most of it in check. "Fine," she huffed, and she closed her eyes. The sights of the park disappeared, but her other senses went into overdrive. Laughter from the playground nearby drifted through the early spring air, which played with her hair and ruffled the sleeves of her shirt. She felt Noah move closer behind her, and his body heat seeped through her clothes as he pressed his chest against her back.

His left hand drifted down the outside of her arm, and when he reached her wrist, he turned it over—palm up—and laid it across the top of her leg. Then he held something against her skin just below the joint. "This will be cold," he warned, and a moment later he wiped what felt like ice water across her arm.

A tattoo! He was giving her a temporary tattoo!

Olivia's eyes flew open and darted down to the white square on her arm where an image was now barely visible through the wet paper.

Noah chuckled, the sound rumbling through her body everywhere they touched. "I didn't say you could look yet," he reminded her, but she didn't care.

"What is it?" she asked, and Noah carefully peeled the paper away before dabbing at the moisture with a dry napkin. She cocked her head in confusion, looking at the honeybee on her arm. It was surrounded by flowers and the faint shape of a hexagon. It was beautiful, really, but why would he—

Laughter rolled out unhindered as she got the punchline. "It's a *honey bug*!" she exclaimed, delighted. She twisted to see his face over her shoulder. "Where did you find this?"

"It's amazing what you can win at the arcade," he said with a shrug. "I looked for birds, but I didn't figure you wanted a parrot in a pirate's hat. If you don't like it, you can wash it off."

Olivia held her arm protectively against her chest, appalled by the very idea. "No!" she blurted. "I love it! I'm going to have it stenciled on my face!"

"That might be a bit much."

"Absolutely not! And you're going to get one, too, so we can match."

Noah laughed faintly. "What if I get a pixie fairy instead?" he compromised.

Olivia pretended to consider this. "Alright," she agreed, "but when people ask about it, you have to tell them it's a birthmark."

His smile faded slightly, and his eyes darted down to one side. Olivia followed his gaze and saw him turn his arm over, showing his own tattoo—the one that definitely *wasn't* a birthmark. "This is a Daria knot," he said. "In Celtic stories, it stands for inner strength and wisdom."

Olivia sucked in a breath and held it, afraid to break whatever spell had compelled him to tell her the truth.

He tilted his arm from side to side, as if examining the ink in the evening light. "My dad disappeared when I was fourteen— just packed a bag, cleaned out the bank account and vanished. Turns out he had a girlfriend with a baby on the way, and he chose them over us."

Olivia's chest tightened as she listened. He'd said his father was a magician; now his answer made sense.

"Everything changed after that," he went on. "Mom had been planning to open a restaurant, but instead we lost our house. I had to transfer schools, and I stopped playing baseball because I was working every hour I wasn't asleep or in class. One summer, I cleaned bathrooms at a gas station and got paid in Rice-A-Roni." His voice changed pitch, as if just saying that out loud was painful. "So I got the tattoo to remind me that what didn't kill me made me stronger—that I can withstand a whole lot more than I thought I could."

Olivia turned all the way to one side, until she was basically sitting in his lap. "You didn't have to tell me that," she whispered, watching his eyes. "I was kidding about the bee."

"I know," he answered quickly, "but I just started feeling like you should know. I *want* you to know. It's part of who I am."

Olivia had no idea what to say. She watched the shadows on his face shift as the lamppost beside their table came on. Then, in a totally impulsive move, she took his chin in her hand and planted a kiss along the edge of his jaw. "Thank you," she murmured.

Noah's eyes opened wide, and she could see questions bouncing around behind them. Questions she didn't really have answers for. One of his arms came around her back, and everything seemed to fade away as his hand landed on her hip, his thumb sweeping across the dip of her waist—once, twice, three times. Olivia became keenly aware of the fact that she was very, very close to doing something from which she might never recover.

"Hey, do you know what day it is?" she blurted, grasping at straws.

Noah blinked, and it looked like it took a lot of effort for him to drag his attention back to what she was saying. "What?" he asked.

"It's Monday!" she supplied, answering her own question. She disentangled herself from his lap and pushed to her feet. "And do you know what Monday is?"

Noah shook his head, still looking a little like he'd been underwater.

"It's *Bachelor* Day!" she sang. She glanced at her watch. "If we hurry, we'll only miss the first thirty minutes; that's all intros and recap anyway."

Noah blinked again and then sighed in resignation. "Fine, but we have to go to your place."

Olivia exhaled for what seemed like the first time since she'd stood up. This felt like a reprieve—though the question was, from what?

17

NOAH: I'm still having nightmares.

OLIVIA: LOL! About the women tell all?

NOAH: Yes! What kind of trainwreck did you make me watch?

OLIVIA: *evil laugh* Admit it though, you loved it. The cat fights are the best part.

NOAH: Not all the kissing in the sand?

OLIVIA: No. Sand gets in all kinds of places where you don't want sand. No thank you.

NOAH: Ha! Noted.

NOAH: I felt bad for the guy, though. Sitting in a room full of your exes while they ask you why you didn't want to marry them is every dude's worst nightmare.

OLIVIA: He signed a contract. He knew what he was getting into.

NOAH: True. Plus he can't be very smart if he's kept Courtney all this time.

OLIVIA: Who would you have kept?

NOAH: That's a loaded question.

NOAH: Nobody.

OLIVIA: Nobody? Why?

NOAH: Because you aren't there.

SATURDAY, MARCH 10

NOAH: How is Avery's art project going? Need any more can tabs?

OLIVIA: No, you've already contributed plenty. Thank you! Please tell me you didn't drink all of those yourself.

NOAH: No, I had help. There may or may not have been a burping contest involved.

OLIVIA: Gross

OLIVIA: The owl looks great! He'll definitely win something in the art show next month.

NOAH: Good.

OLIVIA: You should try to come!

NOAH: I'll see what I can do. :-)

SUNDAY, MARCH 11

OLIVIA: All Lexie can talk about is watching Jake play intramural baseball, and she wants me to keep her company. She says practice starts tomorrow. Any chance you can come hang out, too?

NOAH: Not in the stands, but you can cheer for me if you want.

OLIVIA: Oh, are you playing?

NOAH: Of course!

OLIVIA: Well, good. I'll have somebody to heckle.

NOAH: Do your worst! I'll keep an ear out.

Noah dropped his phone on his blanket and rolled off the bed before heading down the hall. "Jake!" he yelled, but there were no sounds from the floor above. He crossed the living room and tried again. "Jacob Tanner!"

There was a loud thunk, and a second later Jake opened the door at the top of the stairs wearing nothing but boxer shorts. His hair stuck up in all directions, and it was obvious he'd been asleep only moments before. "Is the house on *fire*?" he snapped, but Noah ignored him.

"Hey, are you still recruiting for your baseball team? I want to play third base."

Jake blinked several times, gaping down at him. "*That's* what you're yelling about? Have you lost your *mind*?!"

"Just answer the question. Do you need another guy or not?"

Silence reigned, and then Jake heaved a loud sigh. "You can play if you want to. Practice starts tomorrow at seven."

"Perfect, thanks," Noah answered. Then he started back to his own room without waiting for more information.

"Hey!" Jake shouted down the stairs. "Get your girl problem under control!"

Noah chuckled and kept walking. That was exactly what he was trying to do.

"ARE YOU KIDDING, Campbell? That was horrendous!" Olivia bellowed, both hands cupped around her mouth.

Noah looked up from the infield where he'd just missed a throw from second base and glared at her from beneath the bill of his hat. Olivia grinned and settled back against the uncomfortable metal bleachers where she and Lexie were watching the men's team practice.

"You're so mean to him," Lexie remarked.

Olivia shrugged. "He asked for it. Next time, I'm gonna wear a shirt with Conner's last name on the back just to drive him crazy."

Lexie chuckled and shaded her eyes from the sun as Jake stepped up to home plate. He took a few practice swings. "You can do it, Jacob!" she shouted, and then she turned to Olivia with a smug smile. "See? *That's* how you be a good girlfriend."

Olivia elbowed her in the side. "I'm not *trying* to be a good girlfriend because Noah and I aren't *actually* dating, remember?"

Lexie smirked and raised one eyebrow. "Are you sure about that?"

"Yes, of course I'm sure! I think I would know if we were."

Olivia's friend huffed in an unconvinced sort of way. "But you spend a lot of time texting, right?"

"Yeah, but—"

"And you enjoy hanging out with him, right?"

"Sure, but we—"

"And you go on dates and flirt, and there's definitely chemistry, right?" Olivia didn't answer right away, and Lexie nudged her with her shoe. "Don't try to deny it. Total strangers can tell there's something going on there."

"Okay, yes," Olivia muttered.

"And neither of you are seeing anyone else, right?"

Olivia considered the possibility that Noah might be talking to some other girl the same way he talked to her, and the very idea made her stomach twist into a knot. She didn't think that was true—not while he was still trying to get under her skin, anyway.

"Right," she admitted reluctantly.

"Then you're actually dating. Joke's over. The end."

Olivia's mouth fell open to reply, but nothing came out. It wasn't that simple! There were extenuating circumstances—circumstances that were still in effect until either she or Noah specified otherwise.

And when you do? What happens then?

Olivia reached back and tightened her ponytail, as if that would somehow silence the voices that asked far-too-relevant questions these days. Suddenly, the clang of a bat resonated across the small practice field, and Olivia looked up to see Jake had hit a hard line drive toward third base.

Noah dove wildly to his left, and the ball hit his glove with a smack just before he hit the ground. He rolled once before regaining his feet. "Out!" he yelled, pointing first to his best friend and then toward Olivia in the stands. The cocky smirk on his face spoke volumes, and Olivia rolled her eyes and tried to keep from smiling.

Show off.

LATER THAT NIGHT, Olivia was almost ready for bed when her phone buzzed against the porcelain sink.

> **NOAH:** When I said do your worst, I clearly underestimated you.

She smiled around her toothbrush and held it in her mouth while she typed a reply.

> **OLIVIA:** Rookie move.

> **NOAH:** So are you in for the night?

> **OLIVIA:** Yes. Wild horses couldn't drag me back out.

At that very moment, there was a knock on the front door, and Olivia narrowed her eyes.

> **OLIVIA:** If that's you, go away.

> **NOAH:** If what's me?

> **OLIVIA:** Whoever's come to keep me awake.

NOAH: And you think I'd do such a thing? I'm not stupid. You get cranky when you're tired.

There was another knock, and Olivia finished brushing her teeth before wandering down the hall to see who or what was so important that it had to interrupt her life in the middle of the night. She yanked open the door, fully expecting to find Noah Campbell with his phone still in his hand, but was surprised to find the landing empty. Then she noticed a single red rose secured to the door itself with two short strips of duct tape. She smiled and stepped out to peer over the railing toward the parking lot below. Noah was nowhere to be seen, but she knew he'd been there.

Turning back, she carefully detached the flower from the door and pressed the soft petals against her nose.

Stop it! she told herself. *You're immune to this!*

But then her phone vibrated in her pocket, demanding to be heard. She fished it out with one hand as she drifted back into her apartment and shut the door with her foot.

NOAH: Will you accept this rose?

Her smile grew into a beaming grin.

Okay, maybe not *completely* immune.

NOAH SWUNG THE bat as hard as he could, reveling in the way the connection jarred his bones all the way to his spine. The ball crashed against the far wall of the batting cage just as a second popped from the automatic pitcher. He smashed that one, too, though it went wide and rolled harmlessly down the netting that protected the rest of the Saturday arcade crowd from his agitation.

Hitting pitches usually quieted his mind, but today even getting to beat something with a metal stick wasn't helping. It had been two weeks since he'd brought her back to the arcade, and while he hadn't expected an overnight transformation, he'd really thought there would be something—*anything!*—to suggest that maybe Olivia could be convinced to see him differently, that maybe their game could morph into something else.

But so far, nothing.

And he was running out of ideas.

Noah ripped off his batting helmet and put it and his bat on a rack by the cage door as he left. What he needed was an expert. Unfortunately, female friends weren't really a thing in his life, so he only had one option—but at least he knew she would answer. He entered the number by muscle memory, barely even looking at his keypad. It was almost three o'clock in the afternoon—the perfect gap between the lunch rush and the dinner shift—and his mother answered on the third ring.

"Hi, sweetheart!" she said. "To what do I owe this pleasure?"

"I have a problem," Noah groaned, sliding down to sit on the sidewalk in much the same way he'd sat with Olivia months before.

"Oh, really? Is it the car again? I can send you some—"

"No, mom, it's not the car," he interrupted.

"Oh. Well, then are you okay? Are you sick?"

"No, I'm not sick. It's . . ." He sighed, almost second-guessing himself. "It's a girl."

There was barely a pause on the other end of the line. "The one you call Pixie?" she asked.

Noah brought his brows together in surprise. "How do you know about Pixie?"

His mother laughed faintly. "Honey, you talk about her all the time."

"Do I really?" he wondered aloud. If he did, he honestly hadn't noticed.

She laughed again, louder this time. "Oh, baby, you're in deep, aren't you?" she asked fondly. "I don't even know this girl's name, but I know she loves popcorn, works with children and seems to enjoy driving you crazy."

Yeah, that about summed it up.

"Well, she also thinks I'm ridiculous," Noah added almost bitterly. "I'm doing my best to change her mind, but she still seems to think everything I do is a joke!"

"Of course she does. Why wouldn't she?"

Noah stopped, startled and, honestly, a little offended. "What does that mean?" he demanded.

His mother sighed. "Honey, you forget that I know how you are with women. You hide how you feel behind jokes and games," she explained. "No woman with a brain in her head is going to take you seriously until she knows that you take *her* seriously."

"Well, how exactly do I do that? Because nothing so far seems to have helped," he protested.

"Have you *told her*?"

Noah felt his stomach start to twist into a knot. "Told her what?" he hedged.

"Told her *how you feel*?" she asked, emphasizing each word.

Noah flicked dirt off the knee of his jeans and didn't answer right away. "Sort of," he mumbled.

"Baby, 'sort of' isn't going to cut it this time," his mother said. "Smart girls don't want 'sort of,' they want to know exactly where they stand and why. They want to know they aren't just part of the crowd, that they would be safe with you. *Tell her*," she insisted.

The knot in Noah's gut got tighter, and he shifted on the concrete. Just the idea of *telling* Olivia what he was thinking made him antsy. "But what if she doesn't like what I have to say?" he asked.

"That is the risk you take, sweetheart," she said gently. "That's the price of falling in love."

Noah's protests came to a screeching halt and his mind narrowed to a single point of thought.

Love.

He hadn't used that word in his own mind yet, but when his mother said it out loud, it felt right.

"Just talk to her, honey," his mother went on, filling the silence. "If you want her heart, you have to trust her with yours."

Noah took a long, unsteady breath and dragged a hand back through his hair. "Thanks, Mom," he said.

"Of course, sweetheart. Good luck, and I love you," she replied.

"Love you, too," he answered, and then she was gone.

Noah set his phone on the pavement and stared up at the March sky, where the cold gray of winter had finally given way to the bright blue of early spring. He wanted Olivia to choose him, even when she didn't have to. He wanted her to know that he was serious, that things had changed. He'd tried everything he could think of . . . everything short of actually laying his cards on the table.

But maybe that was the only thing left to do.

18

OLIVIA HUNG UP the phone and did another happy-scream into the empty air of her apartment. A familiar blue-and-gold crest stared up at her from the envelope on her bedspread, and she snatched the letter from its resting place to read it for the fourteenth time.

Ms. Olivia Cohen,

We are pleased to inform you that you have been accepted into the UT Chattanooga Master of Social Work program, beginning in the fall . . .

She stomped her feet like a child and laughed out loud, the sound conveying both excitement and relief. She'd done it. She'd gotten in! Her parents were thrilled, of course. She'd had to hold the phone away from her ear while her mother had done her own happy screaming, and her daddy actually sounded like he might have teared up. They were probably notifying the rest of the Cohen clan at that very moment.

Olivia fired off a quick text to Lexie, who was spending spring break with Jake's family in Copper Hill, and then grabbed her car keys from the top of her dresser. She didn't second-guess herself as she headed for the door. She didn't try to analyze her motives as she thundered down the stairs and slipped behind the wheel of her Mustang. She didn't even make excuses as she left the parking lot and made the turn toward the highway. She simply let herself accept the unbelievable fact that the person she wanted to see the most just then was Noah.

Noah, who had been leaving random flowers on the hood of her car after work all week; who had beaten her soundly in mini-golf and then let her drag him onstage at a karaoke bar; who had eaten the seafood alfredo she'd made without mentioning that it was terribly oversalted. Noah, who had somehow become her go-to person on heavy days and the first one she texted in the mornings.

She raced down the almost-empty streets of a college town that had been temporarily abandoned by half its inhabitants, leaving only those students who had to work or who simply had nowhere else to go. Olivia and Noah both fell into the first category, a fact that had brought them together for part of every day that week.

Olivia laid down on the horn as she pulled into his driveway. It was after ten in the morning; if Noah wasn't awake, then he should be. Sure enough, his tall frame appeared in the garage moments after she came to a stop, his T-shirt and sweatpants still rumpled from sleep.

"Are we under siege?!" he yelled from the gloomy interior, but Olivia barely let him finish.

"I GOT INTO UT!" she screamed, bailing out of the car with her letter in hand.

"You're kidding!" he replied. He might have had more to say, but Olivia launched herself into the air and wrapped herself around him like a monkey in a tree. Noah staggered back a step but didn't fall.

"I got into UT! In Chattanooga!" she shouted again. She shoved the sheet of paper in his face, and he took it with the hand that wasn't holding her up.

"For this fall?" he asked, his eyes scanning across the words.

"Yes!"

Noah's face woke up all at once, and a blazing smile coursed across it like wildfire. He let out a whoop that lacked words but spoke volumes, and Olivia clutched his neck as he whirled her around in circles. "That's amazing, Pix!" he gushed when he came to a stop. "I have bad news, though."

Olivia leaned back for a better look at his face. "Oh? And what's that?" she asked.

"I'm gonna be in Chattanooga's physical therapy program in August," he answered.

Now it was Olivia's turn to be dumbstruck. "You're kidding!" she cried, echoing his words from a minute before, but Noah shook his head.

"No. Not kidding."

"You're *following* me?" she exclaimed, finally disentangling herself and letting her feet fall to the concrete floor. She tried to act dismayed but failed miserably.

They would both be in Chattanooga in the fall. What were the odds?

And who would have thought she'd be okay with it?

His smile only grew wider. "Actually, I was accepted in November, so technically *you're* following *me*," he pointed out.

"I would never do that!"

"And yet you are."

Olivia shook her head and moved past him toward the kitchen door before letting herself in without asking. For some reason, she couldn't stop smiling. "Okay, but you can't tell anybody that. They'll definitely start to think I like you, and I'd hate for people to get the wrong idea," she quipped.

Noah followed her into the house, which was marginally cleaner this week since Conner wasn't home. The sink was empty, at least, and the table wasn't piled high with old pizza boxes. In fact, it didn't look like he'd even had breakfast yet.

"What were you doing before I got here?" she asked suddenly. She whirled around in time to see the sheepish look on his face.

"Umm . . ."

Olivia arched a brow and crossed her arms, waiting for what was sure to be a doozy of an answer.

"Well, I was, uhh . . ."

"You were *what*?"

"I was asleep," Noah answered—too quickly—and his eyes darted toward the hall beyond her.

Olivia instantly knew he was lying. Without warning, she spun on the spot and bolted toward the door.

"Pixie!" he warned, his voice almost a growl as he lunged after her, but she scrambled beyond his reach, bouncing off one wall as she made the turn toward his room. "Pixie, don't—"

Olivia skidded through the door of his bedroom and stopped dead, her face splitting into a huge grin when she recognized the movie playing on his television screen.

"Noah Campbell!" she cried, delighted. "*Why* are you watching *The Princess Bride* all alone in your room?"

He raked his hand through his dark hair and glanced toward the ceiling. "It was just on, alright? We only have so many channels."

"And you stopped on this one?" she asked, watching as the Dread Pirate Roberts struggled to climb a sheer cliff face.

"A decision I now deeply regret," Noah muttered, but Olivia ignored him. Instead, she yanked his comforter up to cover the bare sheets and settled herself on top. Then she patted the space next to her and reached for the remote.

"Well? Aren't you going to finish it?" she asked. "I warn you though, I can basically quote this whole thing."

The mattress sagged slightly as he sat down beside her. "I take it you're staying?" he asked.

Olivia turned to him, a dubious expression on her face. "Did you want me to leave?"

"No! I just have to go to work in a little while."

"Again? Did you have any days off this week?"

Noah shrugged and bent one leg at the knee. "Extra hours are extra hours," he replied. "It's a short shift today, though; I'm only covering for Jamison from noon to four."

"Alright, well, just kick me out when you need me to go," she compromised, and she turned up the volume until Inigo Montoya's most iconic lines filled the room.

"I wouldn't have pegged you as a *Princess Bride* fan," Noah remarked.

Olivia huffed out a laugh. "This is my mom's favorite movie, so I've seen it a thousand times. It's one of those things you learn to love for nostalgia's sake—plus, what woman doesn't like a good 'as you wish' from time to time?"

He chuckled. "'As you wish?' That's all it takes?"

"Well, it certainly doesn't hurt."

The bed creaked as Noah shifted, and Olivia smiled when she felt his shoulder press against hers. She really shouldn't be this comfortable sitting on his bed with him alone in his house; this is the exact situation she would have avoided like the plague a few months ago.

And yet, here they were.

Some time later, he got up and gathered clothes from his dresser before heading down the hall, and Olivia heard the shower start. She stayed safely in his room until he returned, already dressed in his Watson's uniform.

"You can hang out here and wait for me, if you want," he offered. "Or if that's weird you could come back later. Your call."

Olivia considered the options. "Aren't you afraid I'll snoop if you leave me here unsupervised?" she asked.

"Oh, I'm sure you will, but whatever you find is your fault," he warned. He retrieved his wallet from the bedside table and slipped it into the back pocket of his pants. "Want me to cook when I get back? I have burgers."

"Sure!" Olivia agreed. She watched him step into his shoes and buckle his belt. For some reason, those little things felt strangely intimate, even though he was fully dressed.

"Alright, four hours," he said on a sigh. He double-checked his pockets and headed for the hall. "Make yourself at home, Pix!" he called back. "Lock the door behind you if you leave."

Olivia grunted in reply, though she was sure he couldn't hear her. She sat still while the door to the garage snapped shut, and the wheezy whine of his ancient car told her he was backing out of the driveway. But then, the house was quiet, save for the sounds of her movie and the pop of something that was probably the pipes.

It was weird to be in someone else's space when that someone else wasn't present. After a few minutes, she climbed off the bed and looked around, taking in her surroundings with unfiltered curiosity. She wouldn't actually invade his privacy—she *did* have limits, after all—but anything he'd left out in plain sight was fair game.

She wandered slowly around the room, looking at the pieces of paper tacked to the walls: his UTC acceptance letter, a reminder to register for graduation, a birthday card from his mom. There were three sizeable holes in the drywall, and Olivia remembered his story about finding a Bluetooth speaker Conner had hidden along the baseboard.

Then she moved toward a chest of drawers covered in sheets of paper—syllabi, study guides, assignment outlines—and a stack of textbooks took up the entirety of his desktop. The books were thick, not a single paperback among them, and Olivia read titles like *Clinical Psychomotor Skills*, *Experimental Psychology and Human Agency*, and *Medical Vocabulary*. She trailed her fingers along the spines as she read. Then she scanned a piece of paper beside the stack: his entire month's work schedule. There was a block of time on almost every day, often lasting late into the night.

How does he have time for anything else? she wondered. *How does he have time for* me?

He makes *time*, her mind replied, and she realized it was right. It was a humbling thought, and for the first time, she felt bad about wasting so much of his semester with her stupid game. But it hadn't felt like a game all week. It hadn't felt like a challenge to raise the stakes as high as they could go.

It had felt . . . real. Intentional. Like something had changed. Something she wasn't sure she was ready for.

OLIVIA WAS WATCHING *Gone in Sixty Seconds* when she heard Noah's car pull into the driveway and shut off. Moments later, the door from the garage clicked open, and footsteps sounded on the kitchen linoleum.

"Pixie?" he called.

"In here," she answered, turning down the volume on the television.

Noah drifted into his room and flopped face-first onto the mattress beside her. A long groan reverberated through the material.

"Bad shift, huh?" she asked.

He mumbled something that got lost in translation.

"What was that?"

Noah sighed and turned his head to one side, his eyes still closed as he folded his arms beneath his cheek. "A guy came in as high as a kite and wanted to buy forty-seven tiny bags of Cheetos," he said.

Olivia blinked. That was the most random answer he could have given. "Is that a problem?" she asked.

"It is when you can only find forty-three bags in the whole store," he muttered.

Olivia winced. "I take it big bags weren't an option?"

"Big bags have 'government air,' whatever that is."

Olivia laughed softly and reached out to run her hand through his hair. It wasn't really a calculated decision—just something that felt right. "Who knew there were so many nuts in Willow Creek? It seems like such a normal town," she observed.

Noah groaned again, though this time, it sounded more like pleasure than pain. Olivia kept her fingertips moving across his scalp.

"They come for the samples," he mumbled. "Like stray cats."

She looked fondly down at where his hair was slipping through her fingers. "Well, the semester is almost over; there's light at the end of the tunnel," she assured him.

He chuckled dryly. "Are you sure it's daylight? Because it feels like a train."

Olivia didn't answer, turning her attention back to the movie instead. Her hand kept moving almost absentmindedly, and she gradually realized he hadn't said anything for a long time. In fact, he hadn't moved at all. She looked down and saw his back rise and fall in a slow, even rhythm, his eyes closed and the stress gone from his face.

He'd actually fallen asleep.

She smiled as his lashes fluttered through whatever dream he was having. He'd been at work for some part of every day that week, filling his own hours and some of his coworkers' as well; Wednesday he'd even worked both opening *and* closing shifts! A swell of emotion rose up in her chest, but it wasn't pity. It was respect. Noah Campbell, despite his class-clown attitude, was one of the hardest-working young men she'd ever met—both on the clock and off—but he never acted tired when she was around. In fact, just earlier that week, he'd begged her to stay at the arcade until they'd turned on the multicolored lights around the mini-golf course, and it had been his idea to have late-night appetizers afterward.

He *made* time for her.

And not because he wants to win, a voice said softly. It sounded an awful lot like her brother Michael.

Finally, Noah stirred. He took a deep breath and rolled onto his back before blinking slowly up at her as if through a haze.

Then, he smiled, and it was one of the most genuine things Olivia had ever seen.

"Sorry," he mumbled, his voice thick from sleep. He cleared his throat and rubbed the palm of his hand across his face—and Olivia saw it.

The blip.

It was a strange moment that kept happening over and over: on the bridge beside the arcade's tiny windmill, in the stairwell at her apartment, in the parking lot of the pizza place. It was as if Noah had something he wanted to say but couldn't quite work up the nerve to spit it out, and she was at her wit's end as to what it might be.

Or, what she *wanted* it to be.

He rolled onto his side before propping his head on one hand. "Can I tell you a secret?" he asked.

Olivia felt her throat tighten, and it was suddenly hard to swallow. "A secret? I thought you were a vault."

"Shut up. Do you want to know or not?"

"Of course I want to know," she replied.

"Jake is going to ask Lexie to marry him."

Oh. Olivia relaxed against his headboard. That wasn't a secret. At least, not from her. "I know," she declared. "I helped him figure out her ring size."

Noah shook his head as if in disbelief. "I can't believe it," he said. "I mean, I *can*. I think we all saw it coming, but I just can't believe someone I know is going to get *married*, you know?"

She nodded. "It is hard to believe we're that old. I think it'll be a while before I'm ready, though—after grad school, at least." She toyed with a loose thread on his comforter and wondered aloud, "What about you? Do you see yourself ever getting down on one knee?"

Noah let out a long breath and chewed on his bottom lip like he was thinking hard. "Last year, I'd have said no," he finally admitted. "But now . . . I think, if the right person came along, then yeah. I mean, it'll be a few years, but . . . yeah. I can see it."

He looked up at her as he finished, and the blip happened again. But just as Olivia was about to shake him until whatever it was came out of his mouth, he suddenly pulled himself to a sitting position and swung his socked feet to the floor. "You hungry?" he asked. "I'll go light the grill."

Olivia growled in frustration as he left the room. There was definitely something floating around in his head, and one way or another, she needed to find out what it was.

THE HAWK'S NEST was crowded for a Sunday night. Noah opened the door and shouldered his way toward a back corner booth where he knew his friends Parker and Beckett would be waiting. Unfortunately, they weren't alone.

"Campbell! This is Charlotte," Parker said, nudging the girl currently sitting beneath his arm. Then he gestured across the table. "And Beckett found McKenna over by the jukebox showing very poor taste in classic rock, so we rescued her, too."

Noah glanced toward his lab partner, who was doing a whole lot more than just "rescuing" McKenna . . . unless she'd needed mouth-to-mouth. "Nice to meet you, Charlotte," he said distractedly. He wrinkled his nose as he watched the display in front of him. After a few seconds, he shook his head hard, breaking himself out of his own thoughts and turning back to Parker, who had obviously lost interest in Noah's presence. Instead, he was whispering something in Charlotte's ear that turned her cheeks a pretty shade of pink.

Wonderful.

Noah grabbed an empty chair from a nearby table and swung it around to the outside edge of the booth, setting it down hard enough to make both Parker and Charlotte jump. Her face flushed almost guiltily, and she murmured something about the bathroom before sliding out of the bench seat and slipping past Noah without looking him in the eye.

Parker, however, had no problem meeting Noah's hard stare. "What's the deal, man? If you want one, go find one for yourself."

"I thought this was a guy's night," Noah pointed out. "We said no dates."

"Yeah, we *said* that, but look around you, man! This place is packed with girls coming off that spring break Panama City Beach high. They've got to go to class in the morning, but they want one more night of fun before it happens. Why not help a lady out?"

Noah glanced around the room and saw that the crowd was, in fact, mostly female—which was odd, since the Hawk's Nest tended to be a male-dominated hole-in-the-wall.

"The odds are in your favor, Campbell. Go use them," Parker urged with a roll of his eyes. But then his expression shifted to one of clear interest. "Unless you're still with Warrior Princess. Is that a thing now?"

Noah felt his chest tighten at the question.

Yes?

No.

Sort of?

He decided to go with yes. Manifest destiny and all that, right?

"Yeah, it is," he said. It wasn't really a lie—he and Olivia *were* a "thing"; he just wasn't totally sure what the thing was.

Parker leaned back and raised a bottle to his lips, an unreadable expression on his face. Then he pointed the drink toward Noah. "Then you'd better leave or get her down here, because this is not a safe place for a taken man to be."

Charlotte came back at that moment and sidled past Noah's chair before sliding back into her spot beside Parker. Noah's friend gave him one final nod, a clear "see you later," before giving the girl at his side his full attention.

Noah understood the dismissal; he'd given it himself a time or two. He didn't take it personally, but he also wasn't pleased. He'd worked most of the day, had worked all week while his friends were off having fun, and he'd been hoping to shoot the breeze and blow off steam with the guys before classes started back up. But, then again, he couldn't exactly blame them.

He rose from his chair and put it back at the table he'd stolen it from. Then he headed toward the pool tables, at least hoping to snag a game from someone. Music thumped in his ears as he drew closer to the pool hall's ancient jukebox, and he turned sideways to squeeze past a couple who were rocking out to Ozzy's "Crazy Train."

Maybe he *should* get Olivia down here. Maybe she'd dance with him the same way. Maybe he could pull her into a quieter corner and tell her what had been on his mind all week. Maybe it would be easier if they weren't all alone.

He stepped into an empty pocket of space and pulled out his phone before firing off a quick message.

NOAH: I'm at the Hawk's Nest, and it's insane down here. I think everyone in town decided to come dance tonight.

He realized after he sent it that it wasn't actually an invitation, but for some reason he left it that way. Part of him wanted to see if she'd come anyway, just to seek him out. If she did, maybe that would mean she wanted to be with him, too.

Putting his phone away, he looked up and saw his friend Carson racking a set of pool balls on the nearest table. Both cue sticks leaned against his leg, which either meant he already had a partner or he was being choosy about who claimed it. Noah decided to throw his hat in the ring.

"Hey, man!" he called as he came closer. "You playing with someone?"

"You, if you want it," Carson called back. He lifted the second stick from the floor and held it out to Noah, who took it and retrieved a cube of chalk from the corner of the table. He rubbed the block against the tip of the stick while Carson finished prepping the balls. Then, he nodded toward his friend.

"You break," he said.

The game went back and forth for nearly an hour, progress frequently impeded by the press of people on all sides. Finally, Carson sank his last stripe and the eight ball in one swift move, and Noah conceded defeat.

"Good game, man," he shouted over the music. Carson nodded, and Noah felt a tap on his shoulder. A guy he didn't recognize was claiming the next game, and Noah handed over his cue stick without complaint. Then, he checked his phone. Disappointment washed over him when there were no new messages. Maybe Olivia was busy. Her own friends were probably back in town, after all; he wasn't her only option anymore—which probably answered all his questions for him.

He was heading back toward the restaurant side of the room when a small body crashed into his side. "Oh, sorry," he said, though it hadn't actually been his fault. He reached out to steady the girl before she fell, and it took him a moment to realize it was Misty from the bakery, wearing more makeup and less fabric than he'd ever seen on her before. In one swift assessment, he decided she was several drinks south of sober.

Misty smiled and tightened her hand around his arm. "Hi, Noah!" she gushed, a little too excited. "You wanna dance?"

With Misty? No.

A group of rowdy frat boys jostled past, and Noah instinctively guided her toward the wall of the pool room, where a cubbyhole beside the water fountain allowed them space to stand without being trampled. She swayed on the spot, and he kept hold of her arms in case she toppled over.

"Misty? Do you have a ride?" he asked, shouting over the music.

"What?" she called back.

Noah shook his head in aggravation, then he leaned in so maybe she'd hear him better. "I asked if you have a ride," he repeated.

She batted her eyes and grabbed the collar of his shirt in both hands. "Why? Do you wanna take me home?" she asked. Several of the words slurred together, but Noah got the gist.

"You should probably sleep this off," he told her. "Do you have friends here?"

"You're here," she whined, "but you won't dance with me!" She stomped one high-heeled shoe, which slipped out from under her.

Noah caught her with one arm before she hit the floor. "Alright, alright, easy there," he said, righting her again. She anchored her arms around his neck, and he gave up all hope of peeling her off—at least, not before he could find someone trustworthy to leave her with. He looked around the room again, trying to analyze the faces of the people playing pool, but he didn't recognize anyone on this side of the room.

Across the dance floor, closer to the bar, he spotted Parker, recognizable because the back of his shirt had his last name emblazoned across the shoulders. Suddenly, a girl stepped out from beyond him, and every gear in Noah's brain ground to a halt as her gaze connected with his. It was Olivia.

STUPID, STUPID, STUPID!

Olivia berated herself as she wrestled with the lock on her front door. She could barely remember the drive home, could barely remember anything but the guilty look on Noah's face when she'd caught him with some blonde pressed up against the wall in the pool room.

What were you thinking?! she demanded. *He didn't actually ask you to come!*

She finally wrenched the door open and let it smash against the drywall on the other side, only vaguely hoping the impact wouldn't leave a hole. Then, she slammed it behind her again. The motion soothed an innate need to break something—but only for a second. She threw herself down on the couch and started to unlace the strappy heels she'd worn for dancing.

With *Noah Campbell*, of all people!

She'd barely finished the second buckle when there was a pounding on the door.

"Pixie! Pix, I know you're in there. That wasn't what you think it was!"

Fire crackled behind Olivia's breastbone, and she hurled the shoe in her hand at the inside of the door. It landed with a crack. "Go away!" she shouted.

There was a soft sound as the door seemed to strain on its hinges, like maybe he'd leaned his whole body against the wood. "Please, Olivia," he pleaded. "Please, let me explain. Just open the door."

He actually sounded like he was in pain, and the tone of his voice tugged at her heartstrings, begging her to hear him out. Though, honestly, that irritated her more than anything else.

He shouldn't have this kind of control over her!

She shouldn't have *given it to him!*

She stormed across the room and twisted the doorknob before yanking it open without warning. Noah nearly fell onto the carpet.

"No reason to explain," she said, her voice too light, too casual, and in direct opposition to the anger coursing through her veins. "After all, we're not really together; we never have been. You're a free agent, Campbell!"

He winced at the use of his last name, and it was only then she realized she hadn't used it all week.

"Don't do that, Liv," he begged.

"Do what?"

"Brush us off like we don't matter."

"We *don't* matter!" she snapped, her façade failing. "Like I said, we're not anything! It's fine! Go add another name to your little black book!"

"I don't *want* another name, I want *you*!"

Olivia stood with one hand on the door, holding it open while they stared each other down.

I want you.

That was what he'd said, but was it really what he meant?

Noah raked both hands through his hair, which was already standing on end, and muttered a few choice words under his breath. "Olivia, I don't know what I'm doing," he admitted. "I don't know what I'm doing, and I'm scared to death I'm going to get it wrong, but I can't—" His voice cracked, and he shook his head as if to fix it. "I can't not try. I can't just play this game anymore."

He took a step through the still-open doorway, and Olivia sucked in a surprised breath when he cupped his hands around her face and tilted it up to look at him—like he wanted to be sure she heard all the words that spilled out like water.

"I like you. A lot. I think I more than like you. You might be the best thing that's ever happened to me, and if you'd told me six months ago I'd be saying that, I'd have said you were insane, but it's true. The thought of not being with you, of not being yours, of not being able to tell the whole world you're mine, scares me worse than anything else, and I'm begging you please, *please* don't throw this away. Not like this, not now."

Olivia stood silent, her head spinning as she stared up at Noah's face.

"That wasn't what you think it was."

If there was a legitimate reason for the compromising position she'd found him in, then he was serious when he'd said . . .

But did she want him to be serious?

Olivia tried to take a full breath and somehow found she couldn't. Five seconds ago, she'd been angry, but now . . . now she didn't know what she was.

"Liv?" he asked at last.

She shook her head, suddenly needing to put as much space between them as possible so she could think. She reached up and pulled his hands away from her face before stepping backwards. "You need to go," she managed, though every word felt sharp in her throat.

"Go? But—"

"Just, go! Please!" She was desperate now—for space, for air, for clarity. Nothing seemed to make sense all of a sudden. Noah's stricken expression clawed at her heart, and she felt a gash rip wide open when he stepped away.

"Liv," he rasped as he reached the threshold. "Liv, please, just give me a real chance. That's all I want—just one real chance."

Olivia tried to shake her head as she shut the door in his face, though in hindsight she wasn't sure if she was saying *yes* or *no*.

19

NOAH LOOKED TOWARD the bleachers with a lump in his chest. They were sparsely filled, mostly with the girlfriends and bored roommates of the guys on the field. Lexie was there of course, sitting alone along the third-base line wearing one of Jake's baseball caps. Olivia, however, was nowhere to be seen—but that wasn't surprising. It had been a week, and honestly, there was a piece of Noah that would be surprised if he ever spoke to her again.

And then there was another piece that knew he'd go crazy soon if he didn't.

He'd thought about orchestrating some kind of "grand gesture," but he also understood Olivia well enough to know that the more he pushed, the harder she'd dig her heels in. So, instead, he'd sent one message explaining the Misty situation and forced himself to leave it at that.

She hadn't replied.

Noah glanced at the empty space beside Lexie again, and Olivia's question from so many months ago resurfaced in his mind.

"What if we go on a whole bunch of dates and you fall desperately in love with me and then I break your heart into five thousand tiny little pieces? Wouldn't you want to skip that?"

He sighed and squeezed the bridge of his nose, trying to ward off his headache. Maybe she'd been right. Maybe he should've simply skipped ahead.

OLIVIA ARRIVED NEAR the end of the game and sat beside her best friend on the hard, metal bleachers. She wasn't completely sure why she was there, and a piece of her wished she hadn't dragged herself out to watch—especially when Noah was playing so badly. He missed his second catch in a row, and Olivia groaned. "Has he caught *anything?*" she griped.

"He was fine before you got here. Maybe he can feel you glaring at him," Lexie replied dryly.

"Or *maybe* he can't concentrate because those girls over there won't shut up," Olivia growled. She gave an evil side-eye to a cluster of young women near the fence who were making no secret about why they were there. She'd been listening to their not-so-hushed conversation for fifteen minutes and had heard several of the players—including Noah—mentioned by name more than once. The harpies were obviously window shopping.

They aren't for sale! Olivia wanted to shout, but she restrained herself.

"Where did they even come from?" she snapped instead. "It's like he has an entourage. I bet he thinks he's—"

"Stop!" Lexie barked. Her unusually harsh tone cut Olivia off mid-sentence. "You've spent the last eight days doing nothing but complaining about Noah," Lexie went on. "At this point, you're just making things up to make yourself feel better, and I don't want to hear it." She pointed across the field to where Noah stood. "He hasn't done a thing wrong, and from what I heard, you're the one who shut him down. So if you feel guilty, that's on you."

Olivia did a mental double take. "From what you *heard*?" she demanded.

"I was there, Liv! I was in my room when you got home, but I didn't have a chance to come out before he started banging on the door. I figured it was better to be discreet than to announce my presence right in the middle of everything."

Olivia stared slack-jawed at this revelation.

Lexie had the grace to blush under her best friend's accusing glare. "I would have told you sooner, but you haven't been in a listening mood," she confessed. "The point is that you're coming up with reasons to push him away just so you won't have to admit you were wrong, and you're making yourself and everyone around you miserable. And as for those girls?" She nodded her head toward the fence. "You can't complain if you don't stake your claim—but if you don't, someone else will."

Olivia felt both shock and awe at this outburst. Lexie had never spoken her mind like that before! Maybe Olivia had been a good influence on her all these years, after all.

Or a bad one, depending on how she looked at it.

Olivia turned her attention back to the field, though she stared at home plate with unseeing eyes.

Was she just making excuses?

And if she was . . . why?

The voices of reason started a debate inside her head, each mounting its own argument.

Because things might change!

Oh, come on, face it. You've been dating for a while. What difference would it make?

Because the year is almost over!

And you'll both be in Chattanooga next year. You have time.

Because it might not work out!

So what? It's not like you're in love with him, right?

For once, the cynic had no response, and Olivia felt her chest squeeze tight.

She *wasn't* in love with Noah . . . was she?

She thought back to how much it had hurt to watch him step away the other night, even when she'd been the one to request it. She thought about the past week and how many times she'd wanted to ask about his day or share something from hers. She thought about the weekend at her parents' house and how she could have danced through a thousand songs with him and never been tired.

He was the one who made her laugh when days were hard and the one who helped her forget why she was angry. He was the one she wanted to run to with good news and with bad. He was the one she leaned on and yelled at and trusted with the fears she couldn't share with anyone else.

He was . . . the one.

Olivia nearly felt her heart stop as those words sunk in. She pulled her cell phone from the pocket of her shorts and unearthed a text message that was buried six names deep—one she'd been avoiding for days. She opened it and skimmed quickly through the part about the girl at the pool hall, but her eyes automatically slowed as she neared the end.

> **NOAH:** . . . there's no one but you, Pix.
> No one who makes me laugh as hard or
> who drives me as crazy. No one I'd rather
> spend my days and nights with. I know
> this whole stupid game we're playing
> started as a way to prove a point, but it's
> more than that for me now. And I hope
> it's more than that for you.

Olivia swallowed hard and read the whole thing again from the beginning, absorbing every word one at a time.

No one but you.

A cheer went up from the stands around her, and she blinked her focus back to the game. Someone on Jake's team had hit a home run and was rounding the bases without opposition—but it wasn't Noah. She scanned the faces in the dugout and finally spotted him standing at the end farthest from her, his forearms propped against the half-wall that separated the bench from the infield. He wasn't looking her way, but she felt drawn to her feet anyway.

"Liv, where are you going? They'll come up here when they're done," Lexie asked, but Olivia didn't stop to acknowledge her. She was afraid that if she did, she might not have the guts to start moving again. Instead, she thundered down the bleachers and hit the grass at a jog. When she reached the infield gate, she pushed it open and stormed through.

"Campbell!" she bellowed, and several heads whipped her way in what looked like alarm, but Noah's wasn't one of them. "Campbell, listen to me when I'm talking to you!" she shouted again. This time, she got his attention, and his eyes went wide as she made her way into the dugout. The men inside parted like the Red Sea, leaving Noah standing alone at the opposite end.

"You are the most infuriating, exasperating, maddening man I've ever met!" She came to a stop in front of him. "And I don't want to play games anymore." Then she grabbed him by the collar and pulled him down until her mouth met his.

There was a second when he didn't respond—a second where she wondered if she'd made a horrible miscalculation—but then Olivia felt her feet leave the ground as Noah lifted her up and set her down on the dugout wall. He kissed her back like he'd never had a reason to stop in the first place, and the whoops and catcalls of his teammates seemed far away as she threaded her fingers into his hair and tried to make up for all the *almosts* and *should haves* of the last six months.

"One chance. Don't choke," she whispered into the space between them, and Noah smiled so that only she could see.

"Stop talking."

Epilogue

FOUR WEEKS LATER, Olivia surveyed the private party room at Barclay's Steak House with a nervous knot in her belly. Everything looked perfect—the wooden tables were covered in white linen and accented by mason-jar centerpieces, the buffet line was set up and waiting for dinner to be served, and all the guests had arrived.

All except Jake's sister and one of his cousins, who were stuck in traffic. Probably the only traffic Cypress Valley had ever had.

"Jake just pulled in. He'll stall until he gets the signal, but it can't be too long," Noah said, slipping up beside her. He'd been keeping an eye on the parking lot.

Olivia fidgeted and checked her phone again.

OLIVIA: Are you close??!!!!

ASHLYN: Two more lights! Are they there?

> **OLIVIA:** They're outside, on the left side of the parking lot. Come in the front door and tell the staff you're with us. Hurry!

She chewed on her lower lip and tried to breathe slowly. This was the hardest secret she'd ever had to keep from her best friend. Well, except for the fact that Jake had a ring in the first place, but really, the two things went together.

Minutes ticked by, and finally, the door to the main restaurant opened. Two flustered young women dashed inside.

"Did we make it?" Ashlyn asked.

"We parked next door, just in case," Brooklyn added. She was slightly out of breath. "I ran the whole way."

"Just in time," Olivia replied, relieved. She nodded at Noah, who pulled his phone from his pocket and typed in a message.

"Should be any second now," he said.

"Alright, they're coming in! Everybody ready?" Olivia called, raising her voice above the murmur of conversation. Everyone she could think to invite was there—Jake's immediate family and cousins, Jake and Lexie's coworkers, Robin and Kate and Conner. An eerie hush fell over the guests, and it was so quiet they could hear the thump of a car door just outside. Suddenly the side entrance swung open, and Jake ushered Lexie in ahead of him.

"CONGRATULATIONS!"

Olivia joined in the deafening shout, and beside her, Noah and Conner whistled loudly enough to lift the roof from the building.

Lexie looked shell-shocked. Both her hands flew to her face, and Olivia saw the glitter of an engagement ring on the left side.

Well, times they are a-changin', she thought, and she felt a sting at the corners of her eyes. This was exactly what her best friend deserved: a man who loved her, a new family who welcomed her, and a crowd of people who wished her well. It had been a long time coming, but life had found a way to work itself out after all.

"Don't get weepy on me now," Noah whispered close to her ear, and Olivia wiped the moisture from below her eye, careful not to smudge her makeup.

"Shut up, Campbell. I can cry if I want to."

OLIVIA WAS REFILLING her drink when one of Jake's cousins sidled up beside her almost an hour later.

"So, do you know the bride or the groom?" the young man asked, and Olivia recognized the glint in his eye. This was a man on a mission.

"Both," she said vaguely.

"And do you have a name?"

"Yes." She raised her glass to her lips and took a sip.

"Care to tell me what it is?"

Olivia tried to suppress a smile but failed; this conversation was starting to remind her of another one. She glanced toward where Jake and Lexie were talking to one of their guests. Beyond Jake, she saw Noah sit up a little straighter in his seat and scan the room, almost like he could sense a disturbance in the force.

"It's Olivia," she answered politely. "And you're a Tanner."

The young man's eyes widened slightly in surprise, and he smiled. He was cute, though a little too "cowboy" for Olivia's taste.

"A Walker, actually," he corrected. "But that's a technicality. I'm Jonah, one of Jake's cousins."

"Nice to meet you, Jonah," Olivia offered. "I'm Lexie's best friend. I'll probably be the maid of honor."

"Oh, really? Well, I'll probably be a groomsman, so you'll get to boss me around." He flashed a smile that at one time might have made her belly flutter, but this time it did next to nothing. The poor boy was simply too late.

Olivia laughed, more at the irony of that thought than at Jonah's words. If someone had told her she'd be head over heels by graduation, she'd have said they were crazy. She still had a lot of dreams to chase before she settled down, and so did Noah, but there wasn't a person alive she'd rather do the chasing with.

❧

"SO, WHAT DID Jonah say that was so funny?" Noah asked after the party was over. His eyes were on the box of centerpieces they were packing away, and Olivia could tell he was pretending not to care about her answer. She placed the last two jars alongside their fellows and bumped him gently with her hip. They were the last two people in the room, the other guests having found their way to their cars long ago.

"He told me I could boss him around," she said flippantly, and she saw Noah's face grow dark.

"Did he now?" he muttered.

Olivia leaned back against the edge of the wooden table and gave him a wicked smile. "Why, Noah Campbell, are you jealous?" she teased.

He grumbled something unintelligible, which made Olivia laugh happily. She reached out and hooked her finger through one of the belt loops on his jeans before tugging him over to stand in front of her.

"Do you want to know what I told him?" she asked.

The crease in the center of his forehead grew deeper. "Of course," he replied.

She narrowed her eyes and regarded him with suspicion. "It's a secret. Can I trust you?"

"I'm a vault, remember?"

"That skill has been tested."

"Only by you," he retorted. "What'd you say?"

She smiled and rose to her full height. Then she looped her arms around his neck and pressed up on her tiptoes to whisper into his ear. "I told him I'm already in love with someone," she admitted.

Noah's arms came around her waist. "Oh, really?" he whispered.

"Yeah. It's hard to resist Conner James."

Noah reared back, his nose wrinkled in disgust, but Olivia tightened her hold and laughed. "I'm kidding, Campbell. There's no one but you. As hard as that is to believe."

"There'd better not be," he grumbled, though she felt him relax into her arms.

Olivia waited several moments, but when he didn't say anything else, she jostled him slightly. "Aren't you going to say you love me, too?" she prompted.

The corners of Noah's mouth quirked up. "I told you yesterday."

"Yeah, and?"

He sighed dramatically and rolled his eyes toward the ceiling. "Do I have to tell you every single day? That's a lot of days."

"It's only a lot of days if you're lucky," she countered, and he brought his gaze back down to hers with a smile. Then his arms slid further around her waist until they were sharing the same breath.

"I loved you yesterday, and I love you today, and I'm *pretty sure* I'll still love you tomorrow."

Olivia raised one eyebrow. "Just *pretty sure?*"

"Completely sure," he amended.

"Good. Now say it again."

"I love you."

"No, the other thing."

He let a full grin creep across his mouth. "What thing?" he asked, his voice full of false innocence.

Olivia prodded him in the ribs. "You know what thing," she answered.

Noah chuckled and inclined his head until his mouth hovered against her ear, and then he whispered the words she wanted.

"As you wish."

❧

Want more Noah and Olivia? Join the Cypress Valley Sweethearts newsletter and receive a FREE BONUS EPILOGUE (with a peek ten years into the future).

Please consider leaving a review on Amazon, Goodreads or wherever you bought this book.

Have you read Jake and Lexie's story, *Fight for Me?* Find it on Amazon.

ACKNOWLEDGEMENTS

A HUGE THANK you, of course, to my husband who inspires some part of all my heroes and listens to my endless jabbering about back stories, plot holes and late-night imposter syndrome. Thank you for letting me drive you crazy for the last thirteen years.

Next come my best friends, Nicole and Ariella, who helped me brainstorm so many things without any context at all. I can only imagine what it's like trying to answer my random plot questions without background details. Bless you both.

To my alpha reader and social work advisor, Jill, a million thank yous for helping me make Olivia and her future career feel as real as possible. To my beta team—Amanda, Emily, Julie, Kallie, Michelle and Sarah—you guys are awesome! Thank you for taking on this project with such enthusiasm.

To my editors, Courtney and Sara, you blew it out of the park AGAIN! Thank you for all that you do. Also to Stephanie, who brings my covers to life. I've gotten so many compliments on the *Fight for Me* cover, and I know this one will be no different! Thank you for capturing Noah and Olivia in their natural habitat.

To my Facebook and Instagram followers who helped name stores and locations along the way, thank you. And to all the dedicated *Bachelor* bloggers who have chronicled the minute details since the beginning, keep doing what you're doing. You never know when a writer thirteen years from now will need to know what people were wearing on last week's episode.

And finally, to Hailey and Noah. Thanks for letting me be your mom, even when I'm not very good at it.

THE *CALL MY BLUFF* SOUNDTRACK

1. **Thunderstruck, AC/DC:** Chapter 1, Olivia leaves Noah in her dust.

2. **Danger Zone: Kenny Loggins:** Chapter 2, Karma has other plans.

3. **Firework, Katy Perry:** Chapter 3, Noah meets an angry Olivia.

4. **I Hate Myself for Loving You, Joan Jett & the Blackhearts:** Chapter 5, "Don't kiss me."

5. **I Want You to Want Me, Cheap Trick:** Chapter 7, "I think about the *almost*, Pix."

6. **Hit Me With Your Best Shot, Pat Benatar:** Chapter 9, Noah decides to call her bluff.

7. **My Girl, The Temptations:** Chapter 11, Olivia's serenade.

8. **Hurts So Good, John Mellencamp:** Chapter 15, Dancing at the birthday party.

9. **I Melt With You, Modern English:** Chapter 15, Dancing at the birthday party.

10. **Kiss Me, Sixpence None the Richer:** Chapter 15, "He's half in love with you already."

11. **It Must Be Love, Ty Herndon:** Chapter 16, "Maybe we could be . . . more."

12. **I Won't Say I'm in Love, Disney's Hercules:** Chapter 16, "Will you accept this rose?"

13. **More Then Words Can Say, Alias:** Chapter 18, Olivia has big news.

14. **Crazy Train: Ozzy Osbourne:** Chapter 18, Noah at the Hawk's Nest.

15. **Say, John Mayer:** Chapter 18, Noah lays his cards on the table.

16. **The Winner Takes It All, ABBA:** Chapter 18, The game is over.

17. **You Are the Reason, Calum Scott:** Chapter 19, Noah should have skipped forward.

18. **Come and Get Your Love, Redbone:** Chapter 19, Olivia storms the field.

19. **Hooked on a Feeling, Blue Swede:** Epilogue, "As you wish."

https://www.youtube.com/@erinchesnutbooks

TANDEM READING LIST

Fight for Me and *Call My Bluff* are the first two books in the Cypress Valley Sweethearts series, and they overlap in many places. If you'd like to read them in tandem, here is the chronological order in which scenes appear in both books. The prequel ("At First Sight") and extra epilogues are available for free by joining my newsletter mailing list at download.erinchesnutbooks.com/atfirstsight. Check your spam folder for emails from Erin Chesnut Books.

At First Sight (prequel, free through newsletter)

Fight for Me, chapters 1-8

Call My Bluff, chapter 1

Fight for Me, chapters 9-11

Call My Bluff, chapters 2-3; chapter 4, text exchanges

Fight for Me, chapter 12, meteor shower date

Call My Bluff, chapter 4, phone conversation

Fight for Me, chapter 12, Lexie runs into Colt; chapter 13, magazine drop day

Call My Bluff, chapter 5

Fight for Me, chapters 13-16, Lexie leaves Tanner farm

Call My Bluff, chapter 6

Fight for Me, chapter 16, the rainy morning

Call My Bluff, chapter 7, text conversation and scene at the library

Fight for Me, chapter 17, Lexie didn't say goodbye

Call My Bluff, chapter 7, Olivia on the plane

Fight for Me, chapter 17, the photo album and Lexie's story

Call My Bluff, chapter 7, December text conversations; chapters 8-19

Fight for Me, epilogue; bonus epilogue, scene 1 (free through newsletter)

Call My Bluff, epilogue, Jake and Lexie arrive at the party

Fight for Me, bonus epilogue, scene 2 (free through newsletter)

Call My Bluff, epilogue, Olivia talks to Jonah; Olivia and Noah are talking

Call My Bluff, bonus epilogue (free through newsletter)

ABOUT THE AUTHOR

ERIN CHESNUT writes sweet contemporary romance novels from her home in West Tennessee, where she lives with her husband and two children. She spends her days reading, writing and homeschooling. As a former journalist and public relations writer, she has had non-fiction work published in numerous state magazines and regional publications, and she placed third in the Writer's Digest 86th Annual International Writing Competition's magazine feature article category. She'll accept third place beneath a New York Times journalist any day! She can be found in her hammock whenever possible, probably with a bag of gummy worms and a book. Disturb her at your own risk.